JACK KNIFED

A DETECTIVE JACK STRATTON NOVEL

CHRISTOPHER GREYSON

GREYSON MEDIA

Novels featuring Jack Stratton in order:

AND THEN SHE WAS GONE
GIRL JACKED
JACK KNIFED
JACKS ARE WILD
JACK AND THE GIANT KILLER
DATA JACK
JACK OF HEARTS
JACK FROST

Also by Christopher Greyson:

PURE OF HEART

THE GIRL WHO LIVED

JACK KNIFED
Copyright © Greyson Media December 9, 2013

Find out more about the author and upcoming books online at www.ChristopherGreyson.com.

ISBN: 1-68399-030-7
ISBN-13: 978-1-68399-030-7

CONTENTS

1

A FORK IN THE HEAD

Six-year-old Jack Stratton sat at his kitchen table and ate his standard dinner: milk and cereal. As his big brown eyes scanned the maze game on the back of the cereal box, he used his finger to trace the route Tony the Tiger needed to follow to find his way home.

At the end of the hallway of his rundown apartment, his mom's bedroom door creaked open. Jack looked up with anticipation, but it wasn't her. It was the creepy guy who had started to live with them a week ago. The guy lumbered out and scratched at the fat belly that hung below his dirty white tank top. "The jerk"—as Jack called him—strutted around as if he owned the place.

Jack swallowed and kept his head down, trying to focus on Tony the Tiger's face. He liked Tony. Tall and strong, he was always smiling and giving a big thumbs-up. He was what Jack imagined a dad would be like.

"What the hell is this?" the jerk snapped.

Jack slid the cereal box to the side and glanced at the milk spots on the table. "I think I spilled some milk."

"You just left it like that?" As the jerk's arms flung wide, his big belly bounced. "You think I want to live like a pig?"

Jack scanned the old, rundown kitchen. It had crap everywhere. His mom was never much for keeping things clean.

But Jack was a tough little kid; adults rarely intimidated him. Growing up in a whorehouse, you learned to be hard, because soft wasn't an option. He ignored the jerk's rant and went back to his cereal box.

The jerk stepped closer and towered over him. "Did you hear me?"

When Jack didn't answer, the jerk smacked Jack across the side of the head. Half-chewed cereal flew out of his mouth, all over Tony the Tiger. Jack started to run, but the jerk grabbed him by the back of the shirt and flung him to the ground.

"Punk." The jerk shoved the chair out of the way. "I'll teach you some manners." He pushed Jack into the corner of the kitchen and beat him.

"STOP!" Jack's little voice screamed.

The jerk didn't stop. Each blow hurt like hell. Jack tried to shield himself with his tiny arms as fists slammed into his ribs. Jack struggled to use his legs to kick him off, but it was like a toothpick smashing against a stone wall.

Suddenly, Jack heard his mother's voice cry out, "Don't touch my son!"

The jerk shoved her into the wall.

Jack closed his eyes and gritted his teeth as he waited for the next blow to come. But it never did. Instead, he heard a strange "thunk." Then the jerk stumbled back and shrieked like a banshee.

Jack peeked out of one slitted eye—and saw the oddest sight. The jerk was screaming in the middle of the kitchen, with a fork stuck in the top of his head.

"Get the hell out of my house!" his mother yelled. She was hurling anything she could get her hands on at him.

The jerk screamed and ran around in a circle with the fork still wobbling on the top of his head. It looked so weird, Jack forgot about the beating he'd just taken and laughed. After a minute of being pelted by kitchen objects—and receiving one direct hit in the face with a glass salt shaker—the man fled out the front door.

Jack's mother grabbed the jerk's jacket and chucked it into the hallway. "Get lost, loser." She slammed the door shut.

When she turned back around, she looked at Jack with wide eyes. He lifted himself up to a sitting position. She walked over and knelt beside him. She reached out and stroked the side of his face.

"Are you okay?"

Jack nodded.

She helped him get up, then glanced at the cereal that had been dumped in the chaos. "Do you want me to make you some dinner?"

She hadn't made him dinner in months. But as she opened the cabinets, her faint smile vanished—every cabinet was empty. She shut the last one and stared for a minute. Jack shifted uncomfortably. Then she turned suddenly and went to the high cabinet above the refrigerator. She pushed some pots around and pulled out a small cardboard box. Her blue eyes sparkled. "What about some mac and cheese?"

"Yeah. That sounds great, Mommy." He nodded rapidly.

Jack ran to get the bowls while she filled a pot with water. He came over and stood beside her while they waited for it to boil.

She studied his swollen cheek. Her shoulders slumped and her lip trembled. Jack thought she was about to cry, which was something he'd never seen her do. She turned away from him and dumped the hard, dry pasta into the pot. Gently, he reached out and touched her arm. She looked back at him and smiled.

As a little cloud of steam rose from the boiling water, Jack got lost looking into the fog...

* * *

"Jack?"

He opened his eyes to see the fog rising high inside the shower.

"Jack?" Replacement knocked on the bathroom door. Her voice snapped him back to reality.

"Hold on." He turned off the water and headed for the sink.

The bathroom mirror was fogged up from Jack's shower. He cleared a small circle with his hand and stared at his reflection. His deep brown eyes were the same, but it wasn't a little boy who stared back at him anymore: it was the face of a twenty-six-year-old man. He needed a haircut badly, and there were dark semicircles beneath his eyes. He hadn't been sleeping well because of the nightmares he kept having about his childhood. Nightmares that had begun to fill his head during the day, too.

He pushed back his dark-brown hair and rolled his broad shoulders. Most of the time when he looked in the mirror he saw a handsome guy, but not today. Right now, he almost scared himself. He quickly got dressed and glared back at his reflection one more time.

"Jack?" Replacement knocked again.

He rolled his eyes.

Is she ever gonna take no for an answer?

"Yeah." He opened the bathroom door and walked past her. Grabbing his jacket, he headed for the front door.

"Please?" She jumped in front of him and clasped her hands together.

"No," he said sternly. "I don't want you along. Not on this."

Jack stepped around her and opened the front door, but she slipped under his arm and out in front of him. He had to stop short. Replacement's petite five-foot-four frame stood square in the middle of the hallway, blocking the way.

He fought back a grin. "You look about as threatening as a puppy," he joked. He knew she could hold her own. She'd shown that in spades.

"Please?" Dressed in a T-shirt, blue jeans, and little fur-trimmed brown boots that matched her brunette ponytail, she smiled up at him. The outfit gave her a bit of a country look. She was a fit and attractive nineteen-year-old.

He exhaled. He looked down at her pouting face and those damn cute little dimples that melted his heart, and answered, "No." He pulled the door closed and walked around her. As he stomped down the small hallway, the thin carpet did little to dampen the heavy pounding of his heels.

"Please? I'll be good. Please?" She raced after him.

"How many times do I have to say no? *I* don't even want to go. Why would I want you to be there?"

The railing shook as Jack thundered down the stairs. The old door swung open with a creak, and he lowered his head to shield his eyes from the midday sun. As he dashed down the steps, he took two large strides, got out his car keys—and then stopped cold. The spot where he'd parked his big, blue, semi-refurbished 1978 Chevy Impala was empty.

Perplexed, he scanned up and down the street, but it was clearly gone. His hands turned into fists. "Who the hell stole my car?"

Replacement ran up next to him and smiled. "You have two choices: you can have a *really* long walk to Rockingham, or you can take me with you and I'll show you where I hid the car." She held up his backup set of keys and jingled them.

Jack looked up at the sky. This girl was a mixture of infuriating and adorable. He huffed. "Fine, but I'm driving." He snatched the keys from her just in case she decided to argue.

Her smile spread from ear to ear, and she turned and bounded around the corner toward the back of the building. Jack shook his head and followed.

"Jack?" Someone called his name from above.

Jack stopped and looked up to the second floor. His landlady, Mrs. Stevens, struggled to lean her hefty upper body out an open window.

"The Dixons finished moving out," she called down. "I'll have the downstairs apartment all clean in a day or two, but the painters can't start until next Monday.

They should be done a few days after that." Her bright-red mane of hair bobbed as she spoke.

"Thanks, Mrs. Stevens. I appreciate it."

"Give Alice my love."

Jack nodded and waved. After he'd found out that Alice was homeless, he'd asked Mrs. Stevens about moving into the two-bedroom apartment downstairs. It was an odd arrangement, sharing a one-bedroom apartment with a girl he wasn't dating. He wasn't sure how his foster mother would feel about it, but Mrs. Stevens approved. After he told her his plan, she called him a chivalrous man in a hard world. Jack didn't think of himself that way; he just couldn't stand the thought of Alice living in some shelter.

When Jack turned the corner of the building, his eyes widened. Replacement was leaning seductively against his old car, posing like a hostess on a game show showing off the prize. Jack rubbed the back of his neck. Her posture was doing more to show off *her* features than the car's.

Jack inhaled deeply. He and Replacement had been raised in the same foster home, but at different times, years apart. Jack had moved out long before Replacement arrived at Aunt Haddie's. And back in the days when Jack would go visit Aunt Haddie and his best friend Chandler, Replacement would follow him around like a lovesick puppy. She had a crush on him then, and clearly she still did now.

That could have made sharing an apartment a dicey proposition. But it was easier than Jack had thought it would be. They got along well. Really well. He liked her.

"And the winner of the 'Locate Your Own Car' contest is... Jack Stratton!" Replacement tossed her hands over her head and clapped.

"That's the prize?" he said dryly. "I won my own car?"

She smiled.

As he walked forward, he scanned the back alley.

Clear.

His years in the army and as a police officer had changed him. Now something as mundane as walking into a new area generated instinctive responses. He could no longer simply go somewhere; he was always on patrol.

Head on a swivel. Look for anything out of place. Identify possible threats. Drive yourself crazy.

"Not only did you win the car, but you also get the company of the beautiful hostess."

"Great," Jack grumbled. "Now get in." The corner of his mouth curled up, but he tried to hide his smile.

Replacement ran around, slid into the passenger seat, and flashed Jack a big grin. As he looked at her still-bruised face, he realized how tough she was. The last traces of black and blue from her black eye were fading. There was still the slightest yellowish discoloration along her jawline, but that would disappear in another week or so.

Jack looked at his own reflection in the rearview mirror. The last month hadn't been kind to him, either. He looked rough. He was glad to get away and try to forget what both of them had just been through. He let the engine warm up for a few seconds, and then slid the seat back to accommodate his large frame. The Impala purred deeply. He gave her a little gas and then backed out.

They rode along in silence until they pulled onto the highway. He liked that about Replacement. She loved to talk, but unlike most girls, she didn't think it was the end of the world if he asked her to be quiet.

However, today the silence felt off. And Jack knew why: she was devising a way to ask him for the umpteenth time whether he really wanted to go through with this.

I don't want to go. It's the last place I want to go. I don't want to see her.

That was another change in his life. Before, his anger and bitterness had kept his mother out of his thoughts. Now he had dreams about her every night. It had been almost twenty years since he last saw her, but lately she had haunted him. Long blond hair, clear blue eyes—she was beautiful, and in his mind, unchanged by time. He wondered what she looked like now. He pressed on the gas.

"Did you get any sleep last night?" Replacement asked.

"Some. Maybe an hour. Sleep deprivation. Isn't that how they torture people?"

Replacement's voice was slightly higher than normal. "I can drive. You can sleep on the way."

"I'm good."

"We can always stop overnight someplace or something." Her voice rose nervously.

"Seriously, I'm fine." He looked over at her and noticed the trees whizzing by outside her window. He looked down at the speedometer.

Ninety-five miles per hour. He took his foot off the gas. *Yeah… I'm fine.*

Replacement let go of her death grip on the door handle. "Just let me know if you want me to drive." She made the offer with a strained smile.

The awkward silence took over once again. It was the kind of uncomfortable void where both people wanted to talk, but neither knew what to say or where to begin. It was the kind of quiet Jack hated, but the only way to stop it was for him to talk about where they were going, and right now that option seemed even less desirable.

Replacement folded her hands in her lap. "We'll just go out there and see what happens. It'll be okay." She gave a quick nod of her head.

"Okay? We're going to a mental hospital. How 'okay' is this going to be?" His lead foot kicked in again. Cars moved over to get out of his way.

Replacement frowned, pulled her legs up in front of her, and put her chin on her knees. "What should I call her?" Her nose crinkled and she tilted her head. "Patricia? Ms. Cole? Patty?"

Jack shook his head. "I don't know. I don't know even what I'm going to call her, let alone what you should." He tried to slow down. "I can't call her…"

"Mom?" Replacement lifted her head off her legs. "Why not?"

"Because she threw that title away."

Jack heard the wind between the Impala and the guardrail streaking by again. He looked down at the speedometer.

Ninety-eight. Damn.

He took his foot off the gas again and moved into the slow lane.

"I don't have any clue what I'm going to say to her," he said. "I haven't seen her since I was seven. Besides, the doctor said she's not all there. She was a hooker and a drug addict for twenty years. That's had to have taken a toll on her. I suppose I should feel pity or something… but I don't." Jack cracked his knuckles. "You're not supposed to hate your mother. And I didn't at first, because I didn't know enough to hate her. I thought all that crazy stuff was normal. It wasn't until I was adopted that I got to see how a mother was supposed to act. And the more I learned what a mom should be, the more I realized how bad mine was. That's when the hate started. The more love my new mom showed me, the more I hated Patty."

"I'm sorry."

Jack leaned back in his seat, one hand on the wheel and the other resting on top of the seat back. Occasionally he had to force himself to slow down and back off the bumper of the rare car that didn't get out of his way. They were silent for a long time. Jack hoped Replacement would fall asleep, but she didn't. She kept glancing over at him, looking fidgety.

"Can I ask some questions?" she asked at last. She sounded uncharacteristically timid.

"About what?"

"You growing up. What do you remember about your mom?"

Jack shuddered. "Sometimes I wish I could forget. Nothing good."

"Nothing? Not even one nice memory?"

Jack forced himself to focus on the road. "I think I blocked out those times. At least that's what a couple shrinks told me. They asked me the same question. There had to be something good, right? I remember slaps. I remember screaming." Jack exhaled. "The weird thing, though… those parts weren't the worst. She was actually paying attention to me then, so it wasn't so bad." He looked over at Replacement. "Screwed up, huh?"

Replacement shook her head.

Jack rolled down his window to let the air sting him in the face. He leaned his head out and inhaled. Then he straightened back up. "There were times when she would have a 'party' with a man, and she'd have to find someplace for me to go. She used to work out a deal with the landlord who ran our tenement. I would end up stuck in the janitor's closet. It sucked. It was like getting solitary confinement, but I was five and I didn't know any better. It was worse when I was all alone—when I didn't know if she was coming back or…"

Jack arched his back and flexed his hand. His chest muscles tightened as he thought of the memory.

Replacement's lips pressed together. She shook her head. "I never realized how messed up you had it."

"Thanks."

Replacement settled back into her seat and put her feet on the dash.

After another few miles, Jack clicked his tongue.

"What?" Replacement asked.

"I just thought of something. I wonder if I can find out my real name."

"I tried to find it online. You're just listed as 'boy.'"

"Yeah." Jack's eyes followed the lines in the road. "It's crazy to think about it. How can anyone not know his own first name? But she only ever called me kid or brat or moron, usually with swears attached to the front and back. Because of all the drugs, she probably forgot it herself."

"You named yourself?"

Jack nodded.

"Why did you pick the name Jack?" Replacement asked. She tried to smile, but Jack could see the hurt reflected in her eyes.

"It was the last thing she said to me: 'You don't know jack, kid.' Jack. To me it meant—nothing. You know the expression? You don't know jack. It means you don't know anything. And that's what I was. Nothing."

Replacement inhaled, but she didn't turn away. She blinked a couple of times, and a tear hung off her lashes. "You're not nothing," she whispered.

"Thanks. I gave myself my middle name, too."

"Aunt Haddie is very proud that you picked Alton to honor her husband."

"Aunt Haddie was the best foster mother in the world." Jack gripped the steering wheel with one hand, looked over at her, and decided to joke. "She did okay with you, too."

"Okay? I was the pick of the litter." Replacement made a goofy face.

Jack searched Replacement's eyes. Aunt Haddie had told him once that Replacement had had it even harder than him growing up. He shuddered at that thought. He tried to drive the list of "what could be worse" out of his head.

"What about your father?" Replacement asked.

"Father?" Jack laughed darkly. "Whoever got Patty pregnant is about as much a father to me as that sign." He tipped his head to the speed limit sign that shook as they shot past it. "She never mentioned him. I doubt she knew who he was, and I never cared."

Replacement swallowed and turned her head toward her window.

Jack slowly burned. He didn't like lying to Replacement, but he didn't want to admit the truth even to himself. And the truth was, he thought of his father every day. The older he got, the more he did.

The miles went slowly by. Jack rolled the window three quarters of the way up. As he listened to the car's tires echo against the guardrail, he frowned at the junk that had collected on the side of the road: bags, old tires, a baseball hat. The hat bothered him. *Did it just blow off someone's head, or was it tossed aside? What am I, then? Could she not hold on to me, or did she throw me out?*

The guardrail ended, and Jack stared at the road.

Either way, it's trash now. Just like me.

Jack felt the familiar burn of shame in his chest. His lips pressed together, and his throat tightened.

Why do I keep doing this—thinking about her? It was so long ago, but I can't get what happened out of my head. I know I shouldn't let any of that junk define me, but I still do. I'm driving in circles, caught in some loop that I can't break out of. I want to know why she abandoned me.

But some things, I guess, I'll never know.

2

THANKS FOR SCARING ME

They turned off the highway, and Jack flexed his hands. They hurt. He must have had a death grip on the steering wheel. The off-ramp led to the commercial section of the cute little postcard town they'd just passed. Homes with manicured lawns gave way to auto shops and supply companies. He slowed down as they drove past an empty shipping facility and turned onto a long, curving driveway.

The mental hospital wasn't anything like Jack expected. He had been anticipating something like a prison, but this place looked more like a school. Three stories tall, the brick building was set far back from the road, and the grounds were surrounded by a tall metal fence.

Well, that part's like a prison, Jack thought.

Jack stopped at the guard station. An older guard examined his license, then pressed a button that raised the bar blocking the road.

As Jack drove through the gates, he felt the low burn of adrenaline kick in. His eyes scanned the road as warily as they did back in Iraq. Uneasiness washed over him as the building drew closer, and his breathing sped up to catch his racing heartbeat. Somewhere in that building was the woman who held the answers to questions he had waited a lifetime to ask.

He thought about asking Replacement whether she wanted to wait in the car, but she hopped out before he'd even turned the engine off. His heart pounded as if he were sprinting, and he could feel sweat on his back, so he left his jacket in the car. The brisk air did little to ease his anxiety.

"Every place has lepers," Jack muttered as they walked toward the building's granite front steps. "They used to round them all up and put them in one place: a leper colony."

"That Bible story freaked me out." Replacement shuddered. "Aunt Haddie read it to me once, and I didn't sleep."

"When she read it to me I got ticked off."

"Why?"

"Jesus healed ten lepers, but only one came back and thanked him. One? Not a good return on his investment."

"I don't think he did it for that."

Jack shrugged.

"But you know, I bet that one leper *really* appreciated it."

"Good point."

As they neared the front doors, Jack leaned in toward Replacement and spoke as if he were instructing a squad of soldiers. "Listen. Don't talk. Stay next to me. And *don't* get too close to anyone. Got it?"

"Keep your hands and feet inside the vehicle at all times." She flashed a huge smile.

"Seriously. These people can be dangerous."

"They could also be nice and just need some help." She turned her hands out. "You told me yourself that everyone's a little crazy."

"This is a different type of crazy," Jack whispered. "There's the life-has-beat-me-down and I-have-a-problem-and-need-some-help type of mental illness. I feel bad for them. Hell, half the time I think I'm *one* of them. But there's also the Batman-Joker type of crazy. And that type of crazy will kill you."

"Well, thanks for scaring me."

Jack held open one of the doors, and they stepped into a reception area at the intersection of two linoleum-tiled hallways. After speaking with three different nurses, filling out two separate forms, and showing their IDs four times, they were escorted upstairs to the third floor.

They walked down a long hallway. On the left side, windows covered in mesh and bars overlooked the parking lot. On the right side, big safety windows looked in on a common room. Jack watched the men and women behind the glass. Some sat on couches, watching TV, or at tables that were scattered around the room. No one seemed to talk to anyone else. A few people were talking in the corner, but they appeared to be talking to themselves.

Twenty-two people and six orderlies. One exit. Key card access. Guard nearest the door has a card. Jack clenched his fist and forced himself to keep moving. *Think about what you're going to say to her and not how you'd escape if you were in here, stupid.*

On the way up, Jack had noted that on the first floor, they had nurses; second floor, they had orderlies; and on this floor, they had giant male orderlies. That, plus the mesh and bars on the windows, made it clear that this was the floor for patients who weren't too stable.

They passed through a heavy steel door. The man at the door was over six feet and weighed at least two hundred sixty pounds. He stood with his hands at his sides and smiled politely, but Jack saw his hard eyes, and knew that his main role was as a guard.

A weary-looking man dressed in khaki pants and a white shirt headed their way. He looked to be in his thirties and was just slightly shorter than Jack. His collar was open, and he wore his blue tie loosely fastened around his neck. His worn-out appearance enhanced his worn-down expression.

"Doctor Vincent Jamison." He shook both their hands. "You're here to see Patricia?"

Jack nodded. "Thank you for letting me see her."

"Mr. Stratton, as I explained on the phone, Patricia has led a hard life. Unfortunately, that's taken a severe toll on her, both physically and mentally. She may not even recall you."

"I didn't think she'd recognize me."

The doctor cleared his throat. "I mean… she may not recall she even had a child. Her dementia is very similar to advanced Alzheimer's. She's gone weeks without even saying a word."

Replacement's expression saddened.

The doctor looked over at her. "There have been a few times, though, when she's been lucid."

She's not going to have a clue who the hell I am, Jack thought.

"We'll go in the room first," Dr. Jamison explained, "and then I'll have Patricia brought in."

Jack wiped his hands on his thighs. His mouth was dry, and his throat was tight.

Why do I need to do this? It's only going to hurt me more. Why open myself up again?

The doctor held the door open to a small room furnished with only a table and four chairs, two on each side. There was a door on the other side of the room, and Jack couldn't take his eyes off it.

"Please, sit down."

Jack and Replacement sat down as Jamison walked over to the other door. Jack's metal chair scraped across the floor, which caused him to involuntarily shudder. Cold sweat ran down his back. He wiped his hands on the front of his pants, but he never took his eyes off the far door. The doctor opened it and spoke to someone, but Jack couldn't make out what was said.

Then Jamison stepped aside, and an old woman in a plain blue dress walked in.

Jack stood up. There had been some mistake. His mother had long blond hair, not short gray hair that was thin and wispy. She was tall and fit, not frail and bony like the woman who hesitantly approached. Jack cleared his throat. "There must have been a mix-up—"

The old woman raised her head, and Jack saw those familiar blue eyes.

Jack had expected her to look twenty years older, in her mid-forties, but he was wrong. She looked closer to seventy. The years of drug abuse and prostitution had ground her body down to a shell of a woman. Her hand trembled as she leaned against the table and sat down. Her head shook slightly with an almost constant tremor.

Jack felt Replacement's hand take his. He didn't move. The woman who had haunted a thousand of his dreams sat only a few feet from him, but it was all wrong. In his mind, he'd always had this conversation with the mother he remembered: a strong, beautiful young woman. As he looked at this broken husk of a person, anger clawed its way to the surface and burned inside him. Time had cheated him of the chance to confront the woman who had scarred him for life. How could the woman who hurt him so deeply and the poor creature who rocked back and forth in a chair muttering possibly be the same person?

But it's her. This is my mother.

The doctor sat in the chair next to Jack's mother. "Patricia?" She looked up, smiled at the doctor, and gave a quick, spasmodic wave. "Some people are here to see you. We talked about it this morning."

She nodded, but Jack could see in her eyes that she had no idea what he was talking about.

The doctor pointed at Jack, and she turned to look at him for the first time. She smiled and gave him the same spastic, quick wave.

Nothing. No recognition. Wonderful. She doesn't know her own son.

Replacement squeezed his hand.

After a long minute, Jack said, "Hi."

Patty's face went white, and her eyes widened in a mix of terror and bewilderment. She raised a bony, trembling hand to her mouth. "Steven?" she gasped.

Steven? Is that my name?

His mother exhaled and let her hands fall into her lap. "You're okay. I'm so glad. I was so worried about you. How are you?" She leaned forward in her chair and smiled.

There was a long pause. Jack tried to smile too, but he couldn't. He swallowed and slowly nodded. "I'm fine."

"You're fine? Really?"

"Yes. Thank you."

Her eyes narrowed, and then she leaned so close to Jack he wanted to slide his chair back. Her breath wafted across his skin in little puffs as she searched his face. She shook her head from side to side. "No… no, you're not."

"Patricia, this is your son," the doctor tried to explain.

"I had his son…"

Had his son? She thinks I'm my father. Do I look like him?

"I tried to take care of him, but…" She spoke to the doctor, but she didn't take her eyes off Jack. "I couldn't anymore. I…" She shook. "You're not fine." Her lips pulled back in a pained grimace. "You're dead."

The doctor placed a hand on her shoulder. "Patricia, it's okay."

"It's not okay. He's dead!" She thrust both hands at Jack.

Jack looked to the doctor for help. The doctor just shrugged.

"I didn't know. I didn't know they were going to…" She stood up, and her chair scraped loudly against the floor.

"Mom." Jack cringed when he said the word.

She moved back to the wall. "I didn't know they were going to be there. I didn't know they'd hurt you. I didn't…" She started to cry hysterically.

The doctor looked at Jack as if to say "I'm sorry," and then raised his hand and waved to someone on the other side of the door, which was still open. Jack knew the orderlies would be there soon.

Jack stood up. "What happened?"

His mother covered her face. "Terry told me to get you to meet us. Sorry! I'm sorry… Please?" She moaned. "You… I came to the pond. You forgave me. You… love me. Why?"

"What happened? When?"

His mother sobbed and pushed herself into the wall. "It was… There was… Right after I found out about *it*. I didn't know what to do. I didn't know… You were so nice. Why would you…? You couldn't love me. No one could love me." She let out an enormous sob. "You're dead. They stabbed you…"

The orderlies rushed into the room. The doctor held out his hand to Patty. "It's okay."

She screamed, "No!" over and over, as if Satan himself had walked into the room.

Jack took a step forward. "Terry who? What's Terry's last name?"

Patty covered her ears with her hands. "Don't go there! Stay away from them." Her lips curled back in fear. "They'll kill you."

"I need to know. What happened?"

She wailed and pounded her fists against the wall.

The doctor motioned to the orderlies. Jack looked away as the orderlies restrained her and took her away.

The doctor ushered Jack and Replacement toward the door and back down the hallway to the stairs. "I'm sorry. I'm sure you can find your way out from here? I need to make sure she's all right." He turned and hurried back, leaving them alone.

"Jack?" Replacement took him by the hand.

"I need to go," Jack muttered.

She led him down the stairs, past all the patients, nurses, and orderlies. When they reached the front entrance, Jack pushed the big doors open and stumbled outside. He gasped for breath, like a drowning man whose head had just broken the surface of the water. He stopped and tried to breathe deeply.

Replacement rubbed his back. "It'll be okay," she whispered.

Jack's words came out as a low growl. "How? How will it be okay? She's totally off-the-rails crazy, and she thinks I'm my father. She just said he's dead. Stabbed. How the hell's that going to be *okay*?" Jack stood up and pressed his hands against the sides of his head. He took two steps forward, then turned and looked up at the third floor. "Did you hear her?"

Replacement nodded.

"That was just crazy talk, right? She's just nuts. Do you think…? I thought he wanted nothing to do with me." Jack looked at her. "Do you think my father's dead?"

3

HOME

In the parking lot of the mental hospital, Jack sat in the driver's seat, his hand frozen on the key. He stared straight ahead and didn't move.

An old man in a tan work jacket got out of the car next to them. He was carrying a package of flowers and a cardboard box, and there was a look of resolve on his face. Jack had seen that look a hundred times. It didn't matter whether it was a soldier going out on patrol or a policeman going on a raid, the look was the same.

It's called doing what you've gotta do no matter how much it sucks.

The man turned, and Jack watched him make the walk to the brick building.

"Jack?" Replacement whispered.

"I'm thinking."

She put her hand on his. "Do you want me to drive?"

"No. What I want is some answers."

Replacement patted his arm.

Jack's head rose up. "Come on." He shoved the door open and headed back to the hospital.

"Jack?" Replacement hurried after him. "Jack, I don't think they'll let you talk to her again today."

Jack didn't turn around. "I need to talk to the doctor."

They headed back to the third floor, where they located the doctor speaking to an orderly. When Dr. Jamison saw Jack, he sighed and rubbed his eyes, then whispered something to the orderly before walking over.

"I'm sorry, Mr. Stratton, but—"

"I only have two questions." Jack held his hand up. "First, what she said about my father—did that actually happen? Or is she hallucinating?"

The doctor looked away, and his eyebrows knit together. "I can't be certain, but it is likely that she was talking about an event that actually took place. Patricia doesn't speak often, but when she has, she's never had any manifestations or hallucinations."

"Would it be possible for someone to monitor what she says from now on? Anything at all."

The doctor nodded. "I can pass that along."

"When will I be able to speak with her again?"

The doctor's face fell, and he looked at the floor. "That will need to be determined. As you witnessed, that visit was particularly traumatic for her."

"I understand. Do you know if I can talk to someone who has her case files? I need to find out her home town."

"That I can help you with. The name of the town stuck in my head." The doctor adjusted his glasses. "When I first met Patricia, she didn't speak for weeks. We were going through an identification game, looking through pictures, and she yelled out, 'Alphie' and started clapping. I asked her about it, but I didn't get anywhere. I went back through the pictures again, but she didn't respond. But then I asked her where Alphie was, and she said, 'Home. Hope Falls.' It sounded picturesque, so I looked it up. It's just over the border."

"Hope Falls?"

"Yes. If I ever got a week off, I planned to go poke around up there."

"Thank you, Doctor." Jack shook the man's hand, then he and Replacement headed back to the car.

"Jack?" Replacement hustled to catch up to him. "What are you planning to do?"

Jack looked up the road. "I'm going home."

4

BE A GOOD ONE

The traffic on the highway as they headed north toward Hope Falls was so heavy Jack had to stay in the right-hand lane. He drove with one hand on the steering wheel and the window halfway down. Even with the sting of cold air hitting him in the face, he had to force himself to pay attention to the car in front of him.

"I have a bad feeling about this," Replacement said.

"About what?"

"Going to Hope Falls."

Jack glanced over at her.

"Whatever it was that happened up there freaked Patty out. Don't you think we might be stirring up a hornets' nest?"

Jack focused on the road. "Part of me agrees with you. This guy Steven, he's probably a scumbag. What kind of man gets a prostitute pregnant? But... I don't feel like I have a choice here. I need to know. I spent my whole life thinking the guy wanted nothing to do with me..." He trailed off as he saw the fork for the interstate ahead. He debated for only a second before switching lanes. As they got onto the on-ramp to head to Hope Falls, he looked again at Replacement. "I need to know."

She crossed her arms and sat back. "In that case, count me in."

After fifty more miles, the interstate narrowed, and it soon resembled a sparsely populated main street more than a highway. Just as they neared a gas station, the low fuel light on the dashboard clicked on. Jack tapped the brakes and took a sharp turn into the parking lot. He caught Replacement with his right arm as she slid forward.

"Doofus," she snapped.

Jack laughed. "I told you to wear your seat belt."

"That excuses you driving like a wacko?"

He ignored her. "I need something. Can you pump the gas?"

"Already? We just got gas."

"It's an old car; I need a refueling plane following us. Just pump the gas."

"I'm a girl," she protested. "My hands will get all gassy."

"Gassy?" Jack stifled a laugh. "Fine," he huffed. He got out and shut the door. Replacement smiled triumphantly and put her feet up on the dash. Jack shook his head.

He filled the tank, then ran into the little station. A teenage boy was reading a thick book at the counter. Jack grabbed two sodas and some chips. As he headed back to the register, he noticed a map rack with a large sign above it that read "Take a Road Trip," with a picture of a highway stretching out into the distance. He picked one up and brought it to the counter. Then he tossed down some bills and grabbed a tin of mints.

"Will that be all, sir?" The clerk looked about eighteen, and his black hair was pulled back in cornrows. He had a square face, and he pressed his lips lightly together. His nametag read *Titus*.

"What're you studying, Titus?"

"Calculus." He gave his open book a push.

On the counter was a coffee can labeled *College Fund*. "What're you planning to major in?"

"Mathematics. I'm going to be a teacher."

"My father's a math teacher." Jack reached for his wallet. "A good friend of mine planned to be one, too." Jack smiled as he remembered Chandler. After paying for the sodas and chips, he snuck two twenty-dollar bills into the can.

As he left the store, he looked back at the kid. "Do me a favor?"

"What?"

"Be a good one."

Titus smiled and nodded.

Jack jogged to the car, hopped in, and handed Replacement the map and a soda.

"Thank you. What's this?" She took a swig from her soda and held the map at arm's length.

"A map. Do you know how to read it?"

"Of course I know how to read a map. Why did you get it?"

Jack spoke mockingly. "So we can look at the *map* and find how to get to our destination."

Replacement spoke in the same mocking tone, except even more so. "Or I could just use my smartphone with the *built-in GPS*?"

"Shut up."

Jack was backward when it came to technology, and he needed to catch up. His phone had GPS too, but he hated using it.

Replacement tucked her legs up underneath her and pressed the screen on her phone.

Jack pulled the rearview mirror down and studied his reflection. "Do you think I look like him?"

"Like your father?"

"Did you see Patty's eyes when she saw me? Something in her clicked. She recognized me. Not me, but my biological father. I always tried to guess what he looked like, but I never guessed he would look like... me."

"He must have been a handsome guy." Replacement pressed her lips together in a tight smile.

Jack gave her a crooked grin. "Thanks."

Replacement typed something into her phone. "It's a three-hour drive to Hope Falls."

"We'll have to find a hotel."

"Really? We'll stay in a hotel?" She sat bolt upright.

"Sure. Why not?"

"Awesome. Can I look for one? I've got this neat app I've been wanting to try."

"Sure, go for it."

She messed with her phone some more. "There's a hotel right when we get off the highway. It'll be around eight o'clock, so we can get something to eat."

"Can you reserve a room with that thing too?"

"Hold on." She tapped a few times and smiled. "Yep."

Jack shook his head. The way she acted, you'd think he was taking her to Disney World.

As he slowed down for the car in front of him, he wondered about something. Replacement had grown up in foster care, just like he had. Why had she never gotten placed? Sure, she was on the older side for adoption, but she was still only like nine when she first went into the system.

Jack looked over at her. "Can I ask you something personal?"

Replacement leaned in. "What?" Her face was so close to his that if he turned his head he'd be talking into her mouth.

He leaned his head away. "A little personal space, okay?"

"I brushed." She frowned. "Hey, I won't have a toothbrush."

"They have them."

"Who has them?"

"The hotel. Can you back up a bit, please?"

She didn't. "Won't they cost a lot?"

"They're included." Jack turned to look at her with one eyebrow arched. "You've never..."

She turned red and scooted back over. "I've never what?"

"Stayed in a hotel?"

"No. This is my first time." She smiled crookedly and played with her phone for a moment before she continued. "Was that what you were going to ask me?"

What the hell am I going to say? I want to know why no one adopted you. You looked like a normal kid, so why did you get passed over? Why did no one want you?

"I'm thinking we'll need... some stuff. A change of clothes. Can that magic device find a Walmart?"

"Really? Sweet! Yeah, hold on."

They crossed over the state line, and almost immediately a siren clicked on behind them. Blue lights filled Jack's rearview mirror.

"Great," he muttered as he pulled over.

Replacement's head bounced up and down slightly.

"Don't say it," Jack grumbled.

"I kept trying to tell you to slow down."

After several minutes of waiting, Replacement looked back.

"Don't turn around," Jack said.

"What's he doing?"

"He's running my plate. You want to call in the car to make sure nothing's flagged and see if everything is in line with the car and the driver."

Replacement's neck lengthened. "You have no idea who you pull over when you go up to a car, do you? That's so dangerous."

Jack nodded. "I wish more people understood that. We could be pulling over someone who's late to get home to dinner, or someone who just killed five people. Here he comes. Let me do the talking." He rolled down his window as the state trooper approached.

The trooper was about five foot six with wide shoulders and a determined stride. His hat was pulled low so Jack couldn't see his face.

Jack opened his wallet and made sure that his badge was visible, along with his license.

The trooper stopped beside the driver's side window. He crossed his arms over his chest but kept his head down. His voice was gruff. "Are you blind or didn't you see the speed limit sign?"

"I saw the sign, sir, but…"

"But nothing. You saw that sign—you didn't see me. Did you, Stratton? Boom!" The trooper's arms swung wide and a huge grin spread across his face.

"No way! TANK!" Jack hopped out of the car.

Tank knuckle-bumped Jack and then clamped both hands on his shoulders. "Look at you, Jack Stratton."

"What are you doing way out here?"

"I just transferred over to Rosemont. You?"

Jack hesitated. "I'm, ah… I'm heading to Hope Falls."

"Accompanied by a beautiful lady?" Tank raised an eyebrow at Replacement in the car.

"Alice, this is Tank."

Tank leaned past Jack and thrust his hand out. "Jimmy Tanaka. Pleasure."

"Alice Campbell. Nice to meet you."

"She's Chandler's foster sister," Jack added.

Tank stood up straighter and paused for a moment. "It was an honor to serve with your brother. He was a good friend."

"Thank you."

Tank turned back to Jack. "I'm trying to get some of the guys together. Are you still in Darrington?"

Jack nodded. "Yeah. If you do, I'm in. Just let me know."

"Great. Well, I'd better move. I'm already late to report in."

"Good seeing you."

"Nice to meet you," Tank said to Replacement. Before leaving, he added to Jack: "I don't know if you get out here in the sticks much, but you might want to slow down. Locals out here are a tight-knit group. You won't make a good impression if you come into town like a bat outta hell."

5

IT IS TO ME

Replacement located a Walmart and some fast food joints about three exits before Hope Falls. The plan was to buy a few necessities, grab a quick bite, and then hit the hotel. Jack made a mental list of what they needed for an extended stay. It wasn't a long list. People always overthink what they really need, but Jack knew he could get by with a lot less.

A little old lady with a blue apron and a kindly smile waved as they entered the Walmart. Jack grabbed a shopping cart. Replacement took a sticker from the greeter and put it on her jacket like a badge of pride. "Where do we start?" She got up on her tiptoes and looked out over the massive store.

"I'll grab some stuff and meet you in the women's department." Jack snatched a second cart for her.

Replacement pouted. "Can't we shop together?"

"I hate shopping. Let's do this fast."

Replacement rolled her eyes. "Why do all men hate shopping?"

Jack quickly pushed his cart in the other direction. He headed to sporting goods first, where he grabbed a duffel bag. In menswear, he grabbed three casual T-shirts and a pair of jeans. He didn't need shoes, but he grabbed socks, underwear, and sweats before going to find Replacement.

She was already headed his way, grinning as if she'd hit the lottery. She held up a tan shirt and a pair of jeans. "Is this okay? They're new."

"Of course they're new."

She looked hurt.

Jack's shoulders lowered. *You're a jackass, Jack. She's used to Salvation Army and secondhand. To her, this is a big step up. Look at her. She's like a little kid at Christmas.*

"That's not what I meant. They're great, but you'll need more. Come on." Jack headed back to the women's department.

"I got my outfit," she protested. "Don't you like it?"

"I do, but you'll need at least five outfits."

"Five!"

"You weren't planning on wearing the same clothes every day, were you?"

"I can't afford—"

"This is my outing. I got it covered, okay?"

They headed back toward the women's section. When they arrived, Jack gestured outward with both hands. "Go, seriously. You're helping me out, so I've got it. Get some more outfits. Five. You need a big T-shirt and some sweats too."

"A big T? Why?"

"To sleep in."

"That's too much," she protested.

"No, it's not. Just get them."

Replacement looked at him with her big green eyes. He could tell that she was deciding whether he was serious. She raised herself up on her toes so she could search his face. He nodded, and she flitted away.

Jack watched her go. She headed straight for the clearance section. But on the way there, she stopped to gaze at a beautiful brown dress with white trim. She picked it up, admired it for a moment, and then put it back on the rack.

Jack waited. As soon as Replacement had picked out a few things and gone into the dressing room, he hurried over to the dress she'd been admiring. He would surprise her with it. But as soon as he got to the rack, he realized the problem with his plan.

How am I supposed to know her size?

He lifted up one dress and held it up to himself. A guy walking by smiled. Jack awkwardly put the dress into his cart, then scooped half the dresses off the rack and took them all over to an older woman in a blue smock.

She raised an eyebrow when she saw the pile of brown dresses in Jack's cart. "Can I help you, sir?"

Jack looked down at her nametag. "Barbara? Did you see the girl who went in there?" He pointed to the dressing room.

"The petite one?"

"Yes. Brown hair. Five foot four. Blue jeans and a light-brown jacket. She weighs approximately—"

"Am I arresting her?" Barbara smiled.

Jack blushed. "What size do you think she is?" He gestured to the pile.

"Oh!" She thought for a moment and pulled out two of the dresses. "Have her try these on. One of them should fit."

Jack smiled and hurried over to the dressing room. Replacement was just coming out.

"Did you find anything you like?" he asked. He kept the dresses behind his back.

"Yes. I've got four great outfits."

"I said five."

"How many outfits are *you* buying?" She tried to peek around him.

"It's not the same. I'm a guy." Then Jack held out the two dresses. "Here."

Replacement looked down at the dresses and froze.

Jack smiled.

She blinked a few times, looked up at Jack, and then burst into tears. It wasn't a little cry either, it was a full-blown wail. She turned and dashed back into the dressing room, sobbing. Jack just stood there with the dresses still in his arms. He looked helplessly at Barbara.

She walked over, patted his arm, and took the dresses from him. "Why don't you do some more shopping and let me handle this?"

Jack nodded his thanks, then turned and walked in a random direction. He was already getting looks from rubbernecking shoppers trying to find the source of the commotion.

What the hell was that? I thought the dress looked good.

Uncomfortable with all the looks he was getting, he headed over to electronics, which was right across the aisle from the women's section. He pretended to look at some DVDs while he waited for either Barbara or Replacement to emerge from the dressing room. When Barbara reappeared, he hurried over to her.

She gave him a grandmotherly smile. "Everything's fine. She's just not used to someone being so nice to her. She told me how you've taken her in and all that you've done for her already. I think it's the kindest thing that you're getting another apartment so she can have a room and a bed. And now you've done this. She's very touched."

"Do you think she needs shoes to go with that dress?"

The elderly woman's eyes filled with tears, and she suddenly hugged Jack. "You're the most thoughtful man."

Jack awkwardly kept his hand out as Barbara hugged him. *And women wonder why men don't like shopping.*

Barbara went and grabbed two different pairs of tan shoes, then disappeared once again into the dressing room. Jack crept forward to the entrance and tried to listen. After a few seconds, Replacement started to cry again, and Jack's shoulders slumped.

"Why is she so moody?" asked a voice.

Jack turned. There was an old man sitting on a chair outside the dressing room. *Probably waiting for his wife,* Jack thought.

"What?" Jack asked.

"Is she pregnant?" the old man asked.

"Who?"

"Your wife."

"No." Jack coughed and shook his head. "She's not my wife."

"Girlfriend?"

"No. She's a girl… and my friend, but… she's not my girlfriend."

"That explains it." The man nodded wisely, as if he'd solved a great riddle.

Jack hoped this shopping trip would end soon.

Barbara came out and stood next to Jack. She cleared her throat, and the dressing room door opened. Alice timidly walked out. Her eyes were still moist with tears, but the smile on her face was contagious. She turned around once and just beamed. She was so beautiful it seemed to stop Jack's world. Jack knew he was standing there frozen in place and grinning like a moron, but he couldn't help himself.

Barbara nudged him from behind. He stepped forward.

"You look beautiful," Jack said. "Please, please don't cry anymore."

"You like it? Are you sure?" Replacement looked down at the dress.

"Yeah. It looks great on you."

"I'll have them ring it up in electronics so you can get going," Barbara said with a wink.

"Thanks for your help."

After they had checked out, Jack followed behind Replacement. She practically skipped through the parking lot. Then she looked back at Jack and stopped. When he caught up to her, she gave him a quick hug and a gigantic grin.

"Thank you." Her voice cracked.

"It's not much."

"It is to me."

6

HOPE FALLS

The Hope Falls Inn was an old estate home that had been converted into a bed-and-breakfast. Three stories tall, and standing out against puffy white clouds and a bright blue sky, the enormous white house looked as though it belonged in a historical movie. The plush green grass that surrounded the house was the kind that made you want to kick off your shoes and walk barefoot. Jack could tell by the new paint and manicured lawn that someone cared very much for the place. He grabbed his duffel bag, and they started down the walkway.

Three wide steps led up to a wooden front porch with a white swing suspended from ivory chains. When they walked inside, it felt as if they were back in the 1800s. But it didn't feel like a stuffy museum where nothing could be touched; rather, it felt like they'd stumbled through some time portal. Jack watched as Replacement spun around to take everything in.

A middle-aged woman with brown hair swept up in a tight bun walked out of the doorway behind the front desk. Adorned in a period-style dress with a high collar, she practically glided as she walked. Like an actress walking onto the stage, her eyes scanned the room, checking to see that everything was in order. This stage was hers, and the guests were the audience. Then she lifted her chin, looked at Jack, and froze. Her eyes widened. But then she shook her head and gave a slight curtsy.

"Good evening," she said, in a polished and smooth voice with an 1800s' period accent. "I'm Ms. Jenkins, and I welcome you to the Hope Falls Inn."

Jack smiled. But there was something about the way she had looked at him that caused him to stand up a little straighter. "Hello. We have a reservation. Stratton."

"Of course, Mr. Stratton. Room 102. It's at the top of the stairs and to the right." She smiled and pointed up the stairs. "The kitchen is closed, but if you're hungry I can get you something."

"No, thank you. We just ate." He signed the necessary paperwork and tossed the key to Replacement. She dashed up the stairs.

"Breakfast begins at seven," the woman said.

"Thank you." He grabbed his duffel bag and jogged up the stairs after Replacement. But at the top of the stairs he paused and looked back down. Ms. Jenkins was still watching him.

"Will there be anything else, Mr. Stratton?"

"No, thank you." He turned away and walked to the room.

The room was small, but bigger than he'd expected, and filled with period furniture—dominated by a large bed covered in a white comforter and fluffy, goose-down pillows. Dark ornamental bureaus stood along the wall, and a loveseat sat to the left of the door. The wallpaper was a bright white with an intricate pattern of green filigree.

If you could travel back in time a hundred years, everything would have looked just like this.

He tossed the duffel bag down. "Alice?" he called out.

She walked out of the bathroom. "You were right. They have toothbrushes, toothpaste, shampoo."

"They do that." Jack tried to smile and not smirk.

Replacement held up a bottle. "I can't believe they give you all this for free."

Jack was going to explain that it was included in the price of the room, but he didn't have the heart. He flopped down on the bed and groaned. "It's so soft. What's this thing made of?"

She hopped on with him. "I don't know, but I'm going to *love* sleeping on this bed."

He sat bolt upright. "It's a king."

"Yeah." She grinned. "Isn't it great?"

"No. Nope. Hold on."

Jack walked briskly out the door and down to the front desk.

"Hi. I'm sorry, Ms. Jenkins, but there was a little mix-up with our room."

"How so?" Her smile vanished.

"There's only one bed."

"All of our rooms feature a full-size Victorian bed. That would be the most historically accurate, in keeping with our theme."

"*All* of the rooms?"

She nodded.

"Well, did they have a spare bed or a cot back in time?"

"I'm afraid not. But there's a sofa."

Jack tried to recall the room. *Big canopy bed. Bathroom to the left. Old bureaus.*

The woman saw Jack thinking, and said, "I can assure you that there's a sofa." She sounded slightly perturbed.

"Lady, do you have another room?"

"None of our rooms—"

Jack waved his hands to cut her off. "A whole new room. I'll rent two."

The woman's eyebrows rose slightly, and her blue eyes narrowed. "We're currently at full occupancy."

He put one hand on the counter and leaned in. "No offense, but is there another hotel in town?"

She smiled pleasantly and shook her head. "The nearest is in Plimpton, and that's a bit of a drive. And I should mention that once you appear for your reservation, there are no refunds." She pointed to a sign behind the counter written in an old English script: *NO REFUNDS.*

"Is *that* historically accurate?" Jack leaned on the counter. "The Pilgrims didn't give refunds?"

The woman's jaw clenched slightly before she spoke. "The inn is designed to reflect the 1800s—"

"It was just a joke." Jack scowled, and so did the woman. He turned and started for the stairs. "Okay. Thanks. Thanks a lot." He wanted to stomp up the stairs, but he didn't.

Sleeping on the sofa won't kill me, he thought.

But as soon as Jack marched back into the room, he second-guessed that assessment. The "sofa" was an old-fashioned loveseat—only about four feet long. Only a child could sleep on that. He sat down on it. The white cushions were only about an inch thick. He rubbed them between his fingers, trying to figure out what they were stuffed with.

Hay?

Replacement stuck her head out of the bathroom and looked sheepishly at him. "Are we staying?"

"I guess so." He tried not to sneer.

"Can I take a bath? They have a giant tub. I could swim in it."

"Sure. Knock yourself out."

She let out a little squeal and disappeared.

Jack sighed and looked around.

Guess they didn't have TVs in the 1800s either.

* * *

Jack was sitting on the uncomfortable loveseat with a pad and pencil when Replacement finally came out of the bathroom again, wearing her new oversized T-shirt and purring like a kitten. She'd been in there at least an hour. "Smell me! Smell me!" She ran over to Jack and thrust her hand under his nose.

Jack was going to protest the odd request, until he got a whiff. She smelled like lily of the valley. "It's nice."

"Feel!" Before he could stop her, she grabbed his hand and rubbed the palm up and down her arm.

He pulled his hand back. "Okay. Enough touching and smelling."

"What are you doing?" Replacement flopped down on the bed.

"Just making a to-do list." Jack circled the word *LIBRARY*.

"Where's my phone?"

"Over there." Jack pointed with his pen, making a glowing red dot appear on her phone.

"Cool!" Replacement held out her hand and let the laser pointer dot dance across her wiggling fingers.

"My dad's pen. He had it for teaching. I'm thinking about duct-taping it to my gun for a laser sight," Jack joked.

"Why don't you just get a real laser sight? Don't the police have them?"

"SWAT has them, but Sheriff Collins won't allow them for field work. I like them, but more as a deterrent."

"I think pointing a gun at someone would be a deterrent enough."

"You'd be surprised. Look at the difference." Jack aimed the pen at her, but kept the laser turned off. He hammed it up, and his voice shook along with his hand. "Stop where you are!"

Replacement planted her feet and jokingly growled.

"Now…" Jack's eyes narrowed, and in his best Dirty Harry voice he said, "Look at your chest, scumbag." Jack clicked the pointer on, and the red dot pinpointed her heart.

Replacement grasped her chest. "Terminated." She flung her arms wide and collapsed onto the bed.

Jack laughed. "Well, we should probably get to bed. I want to get an early start."

"I'm on the right!" Replacement said. When she was snuggled under the comforter, she peered out at Jack. "You're not going to sleep on that?" She pointed at the loveseat. Jack had put a pillow on one end, with a blanket neatly folded on top of it.

"I know you didn't know better, but you should have gotten two beds," Jack said.

"Why? This one is enormous. You'll be all the way over there. Two beds wouldn't even fit in this room."

"I'm fine. I slept on worse in the Army."

"But you don't have to. I don't mind."

"We're not sharing a bed. Go to sleep."

"Okey dokey," Replacement said. "But if you need to, just climb in on the left. I'll put pillows between us." She winked.

Jack took his turn in the bathroom, then came back and tried to get comfortable on the tiny loveseat, with his legs hanging off one end. He might as well have tried to sleep on a balance beam. He tried several different positions, each more painful than the last. Meanwhile, Replacement was already snoring soundly.

Finally, he admitted defeat. He wrapped himself in the blanket and lay down on the floor. At least this way he could stretch out, and to be honest, the floor was only marginally less cushioned than that awful loveseat. He didn't even consider getting in the bed with Replacement. There was a principle involved here. And seeing as how they were going to be roommates, he didn't want to start their nonphysical cohabitation off on the wrong foot.

He still didn't sleep. And as the hours ticked by, he realized it wasn't the sleeping arrangement that was keeping him awake; he had dealt with far worse. No, it was the thought of what he'd face tomorrow that gnawed at his thoughts.

The nightmares were bad enough before.

What the hell will I dream of tonight?

He tried to let everything go. He closed his eyes and focused on his breathing. The rise and fall of his chest slowed as he imagined himself sinking into the floor. His muscles relaxed.

And he finally drifted into sleep.

7

PATTY

When Jack opened his eyes, he was no longer on the floor of the inn, but sitting on a couch in a motel room—the kind of motel he and his mother had "lived in" when he was little. He was confused until he looked down at his hands and saw the Curious George doll clutched in them. Then he understood that he was dreaming. He hadn't seen that doll since he was five.

A little girl sat on the couch next to him. Somehow, he knew she was waiting for his answer, but he didn't know the question. He didn't know the girl, either. She was small and had big blue eyes. Her blond hair was very dirty, but she had a bright pink ribbon in it.

"I'm five." She held her hand out, but she didn't smile. She just waited and stared at him.

Jack closed his eyes, and when he opened them, the motel room was gone. Now he was back in the institution, in the room where he'd met his mother. The little girl was still there though, sitting across the table from him.

"Are you looking?" she whispered.

"For what?"

"You don't get it, do you?" She tilted her head and swung her legs.

"Don't get what?" Jack put his hand down on the table and shuddered; it was ice-cold.

When he looked up, the little girl was holding her arms against her chest. Her lower lip trembled.

"Kid… don't cry." Jack forced a smile. "What's your name?"

"Patty." She held up her hand, and it shook. "Stop looking."

"I need to find out what happened."

Her little shoulders rounded and her chin trembled. "Then you're going to die."

* * *

Jack's eyes flew open. He was back at the bed and breakfast. He rolled over on the floor and found himself staring at the ceiling. He rubbed his throat and gulped for air as he fought to get control of his breathing.

From the amount of light coming in the window, he thought it must be around seven. He closed his eyes again, hoping he might get some more sleep. He felt like he'd gotten an hour, tops.

He heard Replacement roll over. Then she threw back the covers, sprang out of bed, and stepped on his stomach. She screamed and hopped back into bed.

"It's me," he grumbled.

She stuck her head over the side of the bed. "Did you sleep on the floor?"

"No."

She tilted her head to the other side. "You're on the floor with blankets."

"Yes, I'm on the floor, but I didn't sleep."

"Oh, I'm sorry."

Jack groaned and got up.

"I slept like a baby," Replacement said. "This bed is super-soft."

"Let's go down to breakfast and then head to the library."

"What's at the library?"

"Books." Jack smirked.

"I know *that*." Replacement bounded out of the bed and raced to the closet. She yanked open the door, reached into the closet, and pulled out the brown dress with the white trim. "Can I wear this?" She clutched it to her body and twirled back and forth.

"We're going to the library," Jack began, but when Replacement's smile collapsed into a frown, he quickly scrambled for words. "And I thought... you'd save that for dinner."

Replacement's smile exploded back onto her face. She carefully hung the dress up and danced over to the bureau.

Boom. Nice save.

Jack went into the bathroom and took a quick shower. When he came back out, he was surprised to find that Replacement wasn't yet dressed. She had pulled out all her outfits, and was picking up one after the other and then setting them back down.

You have only five outfits to pick from, Jack wanted to scream, but instead he lay down on the bed to wait.

The bed was incredibly soft. He relaxed and let his hands roll out at his side. He inhaled deeply. The comforter's smell was familiar, but he couldn't place it. It smelled like spring. It wasn't an artificial scent like detergent or soap; it actually smelled like a warm spring day. He breathed in deeply and shut his eyes.

"Do you want to keep sleeping?" Replacement asked.

Jack's eyes fluttered open. Replacement was dressed; she had settled on a blouse and a pair of jeans.

"I think I fell asleep." He shook his head and sat up.

"Only for a second. You can sleep more if you want."

"No, no." Jack forced himself up. "I want to get to the library. But I'll warn you now, I'm going to be a bear. Let's go."

Replacement raced down the stairs, but Jack took his time. Sleep deprivation had made his mood grim. He could almost feel the darkness inside him straining to get out. And it was a familiar darkness. When his mother left him, he didn't deal with it well, according to all his therapists and ex-girlfriends. All the hurt, pain, and anger were like a beast that constantly attacked him and ripped him to pieces. And despite his best efforts, he couldn't kill it and he couldn't make it go away, so he dealt with the beast the only way he knew how: he caged it. He built up layers and barriers to bury it.

Sometimes it tried to get out.

Jack stopped at the top of the stairs and gripped the railing. *Why the hell am I here? I never should have come looking for her. She's crazy. Is that why I'm so screwed up? Can you inherit crazy? My father must have been insane too. Who'd have slept with a girl like that?*

"Mr. Stratton?" The innkeeper softly touched his arm, and his eyes flashed open.

"I'm sorry," he mumbled as he tried to get control of himself.

The expression on her face changed from slightly concerned to fearful as she looked at him. She took a step back.

Jack tried to smile, but his rage still burned. "I'm sorry. Excuse me." He turned and hurried down the stairs.

He took a right at the front desk and hurried over to the dining area—a large room with four small, round tables. Replacement was nowhere to be seen. The only people here were a young couple sitting at the first table to the left. They were so close together, they practically sat in each other's laps. They were in their early twenties, and the girl kept her hand on the boy's thigh as they talked.

There was an open doorway at one side of the room, and Jack assumed that was where the food was—an assumption that was confirmed by Replacement's appearance. She walked out of the doorway with both hands carefully holding a breakfast plate piled high with a mountain of food. She spotted Jack and grinned as if she'd caught a prizewinning fish. Jack motioned to the table nearest her, and they both sat down.

"You won't believe how much food they have in there," she gushed.

"Is there any left?"

"Tons. Now pray. I can't wait to try this."

Jack bowed his head, but took a moment before he spoke. "God... I... help me figure this out."

"That prayer stinks," Replacement mumbled as she took a gigantic bite of eggs.

"I don't think you're supposed to rate prayers."

"Why can't you rate a prayer? Besides, you want God to help you? Is God your assistant?" She shoved another large forkful into her mouth. "Mmm, these eggs are *so* good."

"I didn't mean it that way. I asked for help."

"You should say something like: 'God, show me the way.' You're just a tool that He'll use. And, you didn't say 'in Jesus's name.' I always end my prayers like that. I read it. 'Ask anything in my name.' That's what Aunt Haddie said Jesus told the disciples. Try this."

She stuck a slab of buttered brown bread in Jack's mouth. He scrunched his face, but then he tasted it. The bread was delicious, and the butter had just a hint of honey. His mouth watered, and Replacement nodded knowingly.

"It rocks, huh?" She smiled from ear to ear. "Aren't you going to get a plate?"

Jack laughed. "I thought you got enough for both of us."

Replacement pulled her plate closer to herself. "Get your own, mister. I want to try everything."

Jack laughed and went to get himself a plate of food. They did have an impressive spread, and everything smelled delicious. He ended up with quite a full plate himself—although not as full as Replacement's.

When he sat back down, Ms. Jenkins, the hostess from the front desk, appeared at his side.

"Is everything to your liking?" she asked. The look she gave Jack was odd. She opened her mouth as if she was about to ask something more, but instead closed her lips in a tight smile.

"This food is unbelievable," Replacement said. She held up a forkful of what Jack supposed was an omelet.

"Thank you. We try our best to adhere to tradition, and all our recipes and ingredients are historically accurate." Her graceful, floral dress had a slight scent of spring.

"The pancakes are the best I've ever had." Jack shifted in his seat.

"They're made with low-hanging blueberries. They just came into season. They tap the maple syrup on the farm down the road. Did you sleep well last night?"

"I did. That bed is so soft I could sleep all day. Jack slept on—"

Replacement winced as Jack stepped on her foot.

"It was fine, thank you." Jack forced a smile.

The woman raised an eyebrow slightly. "If you need any information regarding the town or areas of interest, I'd be happy to be of service."

"Thank you. We did want to stop by the library. Could you give us directions?"

"Certainly. I'll write the directions down. Please enjoy your breakfast." She turned and walked back toward the front desk.

Jack watched her go. He hadn't realized how tall she was. She was only an inch or so shorter than he was. She looked back over her shoulder with a smile as she exited the room.

Dancer. She must have been a dancer.

Jack looked over at Replacement and smiled. She had some crêpe filling on her cheek. He wanted to wipe it off, but she looked so happy that he left it.

"Can I ask you something, and you promise not to laugh?" she asked.

Jack nodded, but he had no faith in his vow, considering how funny she looked.

"Can I take this with us?" She held up her plate.

Jack laughed.

8

SHE SAID "IT"

The library was set back from the road, tucked behind a small high school. It was a square, two-story brick building with a garden. Just four cars were in the lot. Jack was grateful to see that the lights were on already.

As Jack put the Impala into park, he leaned over to Replacement. "If they ask, we're here to do some historical research. It's a hobby."

"Got it." She smiled and hopped out.

Jack opened the door and hurried to catch up to her. "Just let me do the talking, okay?"

As they entered the building, the stillness of the library enveloped them like an unseen mist. It was beautiful. Old maple pillars reached up twenty feet to an arched ceiling. It looked as if someone had taken a sailing ship of old and turned it over. And the room was perfectly quiet; the air was still but not stale. Jack breathed in deeply.

"It smells like the woods," he whispered to Replacement, but he felt as though by speaking he was disturbing some unseen force.

They headed over to a short, chubby woman working behind a counter. She looked like a cross between a businesswoman and a waitress at a truck stop. She was probably in her late forties, but it was hard to tell with all the makeup. She wore her light-brown hair high and with bangs in an 1980s' style: frizzled and heavily processed. Her blue cotton blouse was a little too low-cut, especially for a librarian. She was merrily stamping books and didn't notice Jack and Replacement until they walked right up to the long wooden counter.

"Oh!" She gave a little hop as she looked up at Jack. Then she gave her head a slight shake and exhaled. "Why, you gave me a start." She smiled with her lips but not with her eyes. "Welcome to the Hope Falls Public Library. My name is Mae Tanner. How may I help you?"

"Good morning, Mae. My name is Jack."

She shook his outstretched hand.

"I was wondering if you could help me," he said.

"I'd love to." She dashed around the counter and straightened her skirt. "Are you looking for something in particular?"

"Do you have a microfiche room?"

"Why yes. Yes, we do. Right this way."

She hurried around a corner, and Jack had to rush to keep up, almost dragging Replacement with him.

"Can't we try to look it up on the computer?" Replacement whined.

"Look up what, honey?" The librarian stopped so suddenly, Jack almost crashed into her.

"We're looking for some newspaper articles," Jack said. "Just the local newspaper for now. I'm sure it isn't online." He emphasized the last sentence, and cast a quick "be quiet" glare at Replacement.

"The local paper is online," Mae proudly proclaimed. "They started to publish online last year."

"That's great," Jack began, "but I wanted to look at some papers going back around twenty-eight years. We're here to do some historical research. Is that on microfiche?"

"It is."

Mae led them down a corridor to a small side room with old metal cabinets along every wall. In the middle of the room was a large wooden table with a microfiche machine.

"We have every copy of the *Hope Falls Times* since they started publishing in 1923. We also have the regional paper, the *Enterprise*. As you can see," she looked up at Jack and blinked rapidly, "we've also… we've also—" Mae stammered and looked down at her hands. "We also have—" She stopped again and cleared her throat.

"Mae." Jack placed a hand gently on her shoulder. "This is perfect." He smiled, and she started to breathe again. "This is exactly what I need."

"Really?" She smiled. "Wonderful. Please let me know if you need anything else." She scurried out of the room.

"What was that all about?" Replacement asked.

"Shh…" Jack peered out the door and watched Mae hurry back to her desk. "Maybe she's just nervous. Besides, this is what we came for."

"This? What're we going to find here?"

"First, we'll find out if my mother is just crazy and if any of what she said really happened." He opened a cabinet under a sign that read: *Hope Falls Press*. The records were arranged by date; Jack thumbed through until he had the folder he wanted. When he turned back to the table, Replacement had already turned on the machine and was waiting for him.

"I'm twenty-six. She'd have been pregnant twenty-seven years ago. We'll start there and go forward," Jack began. "Let me explain how this works."

Replacement held up her smartphone. "Googled it. This reader has a translucent screen at the front, which projects an image from a microform. Three hundred pages per form, so I'm guessing one month per film." She gave a little wiggle when she finished and laughed.

"Show-off." Jack placed the folder down next to the machine.

"How do you know we need to search the period from shortly before you were born?"

"When Patty was freaking out in the hospital, she said the stabbing happened after she found out about '*it*.'" His eyes burned, but his voice was cold.

Replacement clearly didn't understand. "What does that mean?"

"The '*it*' she was talking about was me."

Replacement's face fell. "I'm sorry, Jack."

Jack took a seat in front of the microfiche reader. He started with July, placing the square film into the machine. The front page of the paper was displayed on the monitor. "With a town as small as Hope Falls, a stabbing would be front page news," he said, "but just in case, we should check the whole paper."

They looked through every page, but found only mundane small-town stories about homecomings and elections. So they moved on to the next week's paper. *A weekly paper*, Jack thought. *This really is a small town.*

They found nothing in the rest of July either—or in August, September, or October. Every new page that appeared on the flickering machine made Jack's heart speed up. He forced himself to go slow and scan each page. Replacement didn't speak. She just pointed at the monitor once or twice.

Jack put in the November film while Replacement stood behind him and looked over his shoulder. The machine hummed. They continued to scan through the pages, seeing nothing of interest.

And then Jack pulled up the November 14 paper—and time stopped.

Replacement gasped.

Jack had never in his life seen the teenager pictured on the front page of the paper, but he knew exactly who he was looking at: his father.

"He was just a kid," Jack whispered. *Maybe seventeen. Smiling. Yearbook photo.*

"You look just like him."

Jack didn't move. His hand was frozen on the knob of the machine. He could hear his heart pounding in his ears. "Steven. Steven Ritter. That was my father's name. I was hoping she was wrong. That it was just some delusion…" He tried to read, but his vision blurred. "Teen Killed at Buckmaster Pond" was the headline.

Jack scanned his father's face. Steven's photo was in black and white, but the resemblance to his own high school yearbook photo was uncanny. "It says he was killed, stabbed… That's what my mother said. He was…" Jack wiped his eyes and turned toward Replacement. "I can't read it. Can you?"

She already had tears running down her own face. "Jack…" She leaned down and wrapped her arms around him.

Jack shook. "I thought maybe… maybe she was just crazy. I always thought I'd meet him someday."

Replacement didn't say a word; she just held him tighter.

"When I was a kid and things were tough, I thought he'd come looking for me, and save me." Jack's shoulders slumped.

"Oh, Jack."

"My father's dead."

Jack couldn't hold back his emotions any longer. Replacement slowly rocked him back and forth. Jack had no idea how long he cried, but Replacement never let go of him.

After a while, he heard a noise from the doorway. He turned and saw the little librarian standing there, holding a box of tissues. Jack wiped his eyes and looked away while Replacement hurriedly went to the door.

Mae hesitantly held the tissue box out to Replacement. Her head turned toward the large microfiche screen. "I'm sorry," she mumbled.

"It's okay." Replacement took the tissues from her.

"Please, do let me know if you need anything else." Mae rushed out of the room.

Replacement walked back over to Jack and set the tissues on the table in front of him.

"Thanks." Jack's voice was raspy. "Sorry I'm such a pansy."

Replacement lowered her face to eye level with his. "Shut up." Her lips pressed together. "You just found out your father was murdered."

Jack cracked his neck and stood up. He stretched and walked toward the door.

Replacement's voice was soft. "Do you want to go?"

Jack grabbed a pencil and some scrap paper from a basket near the door. "Leave?" Jack's voice was a low growl. "No. I'm just getting started."

9

ACTA NON VERBA

"On November 13, an emergency call came in, reporting a stabbing at Buckmaster Pond. Steven Ritter. Seventeen. Beaten. Stabbed. No other information. Police following all leads, according to Chief Dennis Wilson."

Jack stopped talking and looked at Replacement. She had pulled up a chair next to his, and was writing everything down as fast as he spoke.

"We can come back," she offered.

"I'm fine." He turned back to the monitor. "This is better for me. Really."

He scanned the article to see whether he'd missed anything. Then his hand turned the knob forward. "Next paper. November 21. Police are asking anyone with information to come forward. No suspects. No witnesses. Steven. Only child of Mrs. Mary Ritter, a widow…"

My grandmother. She was a widow.

Jack's fists shook on the table, and he knew he was close to smashing something. "I'm sorry. My head is going to explode. My crazy mother was right. And now I know my father is dead. Murdered. And *his* father was already dead. My grandmother… she was… all alone."

Replacement put a hand on his arm. "Jack. This is too much for anyone all at once. Let's go for today, okay? We'll come back tomorrow. We've waited this long. We can wait one more day."

"Wait another day? I don't want to give the guy who killed him another *breath*, let alone another day. Let's get a little more. Can you please drive?"

Replacement hesitated, but when Jack stood up, she took his seat in front of the microfiche machine. "All right. Next paper." Replacement began to read. "Here we go. November 28. Police say there's still no progress. Following multiple leads. Cause of death: multiple sharp-force injuries. Police asking for help. They searched the area surrounding the pond, but no weapon was recovered."

"Does it give any names? Cops' names who were involved in the investigation?"

Replacement scanned the article. "Frank Nelson and Henry Cooper. They're listed as responding officers."

Jack wrote that down.

"Okay, next week." Excited now, Replacement quickly swapped out the November microfiche for the December one. But when she scanned the front page of the

December 5 edition, she frowned; there was no mention of the murder. She flipped through page after page, but there wasn't a single reference to the crime. She looked at Jack, but he just stared at the screen. She looked through the rest of December. She slowly turned the knob, making sure she didn't skip anything—but there was nothing to skip. There was no further news on the murder. Replacement took her hand off the dial.

"They only dredged the pond. They didn't even bring in the state police dive team." Jack jabbed the screen with his pencil. "It froze over before they could get the divers here. But what about spring? Did they just forget about him?"

After they went through three more months and found nothing more, Jack stood up. "We've gotten everything from the newspaper that we're going to get."

Replacement went to put the microfiche away. Jack ran his fingers through his hair. "One more stop," he said, "and then we go."

The library was absolutely still as they walked back to the front counter. They passed an area where a few empty wooden desks had been set up—a children's study area. For just a moment, Jack could picture his father as a schoolboy sitting there, reading.

My father would have come here. He'd have…

Jack stumbled, and his whole body tensed. Replacement looked nervously at him. He could see the concern on her face.

"I'm fine. I'm just trying not to go down the 'what could have been' road."

"Don't go there." Replacement's voice was low. "It'll make you crazy. Then it'll kill you."

Her words made Jack pause. He searched her eyes. Her face was stern and her gaze was steady. "Is that a road you've been on?"

She didn't answer.

Back in the main area of the library, they found the main desk unmanned; Mae was nowhere to be seen. That was fine with Jack. After the incident in the microfiche room, he didn't much feel like facing the woman.

He led Replacement toward the non-fiction area. He scanned the signs at the end of the shelves until he found what he was looking for: almanacs, yearbooks, and handbooks. He went down that row, stopped in the middle, and gestured to the section he wanted to search. Yearbooks.

"I can do this," Replacement said. She grabbed a stepstool and made Jack sit down.

"Get all the books from thirty years ago to twenty-five years ago, just to be on the safe side," he mumbled.

Replacement pulled down a few yearbooks. She handed them to Jack, and he handed three back to her. She began to leaf through the pages.

Jack decided to look for his father first. He skipped straight to the Rs. "Got it." He stared at the picture of his father. It was the same picture as the one in the paper, although this one was in color.

Replacement leaned over his shoulder. "You look so much alike. Look at his cheekbones and chin. But your eyes… they're the same. Totally."

Jack read the text below the photo. *STEVEN RITTER. "ACTA NON VERBA" IN MEMORIUM.* Puzzled, he looked up at Replacement. She was already typing on her phone.

"Acta non verba," she repeated as she continued to type. "It's Latin. It means deeds, not words."

Jack flipped to the Cs next. "Marie Drake… Theresa Cook… Alyssa Connery…"

When he came to the photo of his mother, he stopped and stared. She had long blond hair, wore a simple white dress, and was smiling from ear to ear. She was beautiful. Jack squeezed the yearbook, and his eyes narrowed.

The yearbook text read, *PATRICIA COLE*, but underneath her name, someone had handwritten the words, *CLASS SLUT.*

Jack's anger boiled.

"They were in the same year," Replacement said.

"We need to look for a guy named Terry," Jack growled. "She said Terry told her to get Steven to come to the pond. If you find a Terry, any Terry, flag the page. You start on the previous year."

"Do we know if Terry even went to her school?"

"No. But I'm assuming."

They both flipped through pages. After a minute, Replacement blurted out, "Found one." She pointed.

Jack looked at the picture. A young, smug-looking guy. Dark hair and brown eyes. *TERRY BRADFORD.*

"He was a year ahead of my par—of them. Keep looking."

Replacement flagged the page. Jack kept scanning.

All these kids. They knew my father. I wonder…

He shut his eyes and tried to concentrate. His finger moved across every name. When he got to the M's, he stopped.

"I've got two. Terry Martinez and Terry Martin."

Replacement poked Terry Martin's picture. "He looks like a jerk." Terry Martin was dressed in a football sweater with an open collar around his thick neck. Jack took one look at the kid's cocky grin and wanted to knock it off his face.

Then Replacement pointed to Terry Martinez. "He looks nice though. Nerdy, but nice." Dressed in a white shirt and plain blue tie, Martinez looked younger than the other students. He was thin, with a mop of black hair, and he wore thick glasses that were too big for his face.

The book's cover made a cracking sound as Jack's hand tightened around it. He relaxed his grip and continued to flip pages.

They went through all the other yearbooks Replacement had pulled out, but found no one else named Terry. "Well, we've got three," Jack said. "It's a place to start." He put away most of the yearbooks, but kept the two that they had originally flagged. "We walked by a photocopier. I want to copy the pictures."

Replacement followed him to the copier. It wasn't the best quality, but after a couple minutes, Jack had his copies. He began to walk away to put the books back, then stopped and sighed.

"Jack? What's wrong?"

A world of pain I didn't know existed two days ago is making me crazy, is what Jack wanted to say, but instead he replied, "I feel like I should photocopy these whole books. There might be something in here."

"Can't we just check them out?"

"No. See the little sticker on the back? *'Not available for checkout. Do not remove from Hope Falls Public Library.'* I guess because they're unique reference books. But it's fine. We got what we needed."

"Okay. I'll go put them away." Replacement took the two yearbooks from Jack and hurried back to the shelves.

Three names, Jack thought. *How can I run background checks on them from here? I don't think I can connect to any of the police systems with just a cell phone. The chief wouldn't be too happy if I logged in to the police system through a public library computer, and I'm sure the inn won't have a computer—since I doubt they had computers in the Revolutionary War. I should just call Cindy and have her run a check on the QT—*

When Replacement touched his arm, he jumped.

"Sorry." She smiled.

"Let's go. Are you hungry?" Jack asked.

"Starving." Replacement hugged her stomach.

"You just ate that humongous breakfast. How can you be starving?"

"It's already after lunch time." She held up her hand. "But I don't have to get something—"

"I didn't realize it was so late. I'm sorry. Come on."

When they walked past the main desk, Mae was still nowhere in sight. They strode on out into the cool air, and Jack stopped and breathed deeply.

Replacement grabbed his arm. "I'm driving." She pulled the keys from his pocket and darted to the car. "You look like hell."

"Thanks," Jack muttered, but he didn't protest her driving. "I feel like hell."

He got in the passenger's seat and looked over at Replacement, who was squirming around in the driver's seat. Perplexed, he stared, thinking she must be trying to take her jacket off. Then she leaned forward and, with a triumphant grin, pulled two yearbooks from inside the back of her sweater.

"You stole the yearbooks?" Jack's mouth fell open.

"I didn't exactly steal them. You said there might be something you need in them."

"There might be, but you *took* them."

"Yes, I *took* them, but I didn't *steal* them because I'm going to return them."

Jack was about to argue, but decided there was no point. "Fine." He leaned against the window.

Replacement broke into a huge smile. "I'm glad you agree."

As Replacement pulled out of the parking lot, Jack saw the librarian. She was standing at a side entrance, talking with a tall man who looked to be about Jack's age. He wore a worn baseball cap, tan work coat, jeans, and boots.

Mae saw Jack looking. She grabbed the man by the arm and pulled him inside the library.

"Where do you want to eat?" Replacement asked as she headed for the main road.

Jack tried to drive his police officer paranoia out of his head. "Anywhere, klepto."

10

BUTTERCUP

They pulled up outside Bartlet's Family Restaurant, which looked like a log cabin with a wide wraparound porch. Quite a few cars were parked here, so Jack hoped the food would be good. Jack stretched as he opened the car door. He couldn't get over how warm the winter had been. A jacket was still needed, but for the beginning of February, this would be considered a heat wave.

The doors to the restaurant opened onto a spacious front room that doubled as a gift shop. The place had all manner of touristy stuff—plastic toys for kids, crafts, shirts, caps—and it seemed that just about everything was either on a yellow pine shelf or in a pine barrel. As Jack strode purposefully through the bric-a-brac to the main restaurant, he realized that Replacement was no longer with him. Backtracking, he found her examining a pink T-shirt with *HOPE FALLS* written in the middle of a large red heart. He grabbed her by the arm and headed for the hostess.

"Can't I look for a minute?" Replacement begged.

"You can look for an hour after we eat. You're starving, remember?" Jack smiled at the young hostess who stood behind a wooden podium. "Table for two."

She grabbed some menus and led them to a little corner booth. As soon as Replacement slid into her seat, she looked out the window and her mouth dropped open. Behind the restaurant was a small garden with a little natural waterfall.

"Isn't it pretty?" their waitress remarked as she stopped beside their table. "I just love it. It's so romantic." She gave Replacement a little pat on the shoulder and winked.

"It's beautiful." Replacement kept gazing out the window.

Jack suddenly stood. "I'll be right back."

The waitress looked perplexed. "Do you want to order?"

"A burger and fries," Jack called over his shoulder as he marched back into the store. "And a Coke."

He walked into the gift shop again and scanned the shelves. He looked around a little but didn't see what he needed. He walked over to the cashier.

"Do you have any notebooks?" he asked.

"Yes, we do. Right over there." She pointed to a shelf that held precisely two notebooks: a thin one covered in puffy baby farm animals, and a thicker, purple one, decorated with sparkling confetti and the words "HOPE FALLS" written in hot pink.

Jack rolled his eyes and paid for the thicker notebook, along with a pen.

"She'll love them," the woman confidently assured him.

"Who will?"

"Your girlfriend." She smiled.

Jack tilted his head down, grabbed the bag, and hurried back to the table. Replacement was still looking out the window as he slid back into the booth.

"Where did you go?" she asked.

"I needed to get a notebook." He put it on the table.

She snickered. "Pink's not your color."

Jack's eyes narrowed. "What're you, five years old?"

"Me? I'm not the one with the Pretty Pony notebook."

"Anyway," he pulled out the scraps of paper from the library, "I figured we could get started organizing the information we have."

"I'll write." She took the pen.

They transcribed the notes while they ate. Once they had everything written down, Jack frowned. "We don't have much."

"It's a good start." Replacement slurped down the last of her milkshake and ended it with a loud smack of her lips.

"It's strange that there wasn't more in the paper."

"There was at the beginning."

"The story faded out fast."

They were done with their meal, so Replacement headed back to the little shop while Jack went to pay the bill. After he'd paid, he found her once again admiring the same pink shirt she'd looked at on the way in. When he walked over to her, she looked at him, hopeful.

He grabbed a matching pink baseball hat off the shelf. "Get the hat, too."

"Really? No. I don't want to spend—"

"Get them. They'll look good on you."

Replacement tried to hide her blush.

"Come on. I want to make one more stop before we head back to the inn."

"Where?"

"There was a little general store in town. I'm hoping they have what I need."

"You're not gonna tell me?"

"It's none of your business." Jack took the shirt and hat up to the register.

Replacement stopped at a rack of postcards. "I'm going to get one for Aunt Haddie."

"Sure." Jack handed the shirt and hat to the cashier. "These, a postcard and a stamp."

"Did your girlfriend like the notebook?" The lady smiled.

"What? No, she's not..." Jack winced when Replacement came over and pinched him.

"He's such a kidder." Her arm slid around Jack's waist, and she gave him a hard hug. "Thanks, sweetie. I loved my notebook."

"Sure... buttercup." Jack pinched her cheek.

As they exited the restaurant, Replacement whispered, "Buttercup? Come on. You stink at being undercover."

"Don't start the whole undercover thing again."

"What do you mean? I did great undercover."

"We're not undercover." Jack's voice got louder as they walked toward the car.

"Are we telling people what we're doing?"

"No."

"Ha!" Replacement pointed a finger in his face. "Then we're undercover."

"No, we're just not…" Jack pulled open his door and leaned on the roof of the car as Replacement walked to her side. "Fine. We're undercover. But we're not doing the boyfriend-girlfriend thing."

"That's our cover. You can't be undercover unless you have a cover, and that's our cover."

Jack frowned. "We can pick another cover."

"No, we can't."

Jack shook his head.

"What else would we pick? Are we a traveling circus team?" Replacement pantomimed juggling.

Jack tried not to, but he smiled at her joke as they got into the car. "No. We keep it simple and vague. We're doing some historical research. It gives us an opening. Then we wait and see what they say."

Replacement crossed her arms.

"You don't like that plan?"

"I don't like any of this. We're going after the man who killed your father. He's dangerous."

Jack started the Impala. The engine roared. He wanted to reassure Replacement that she was safe, but when the words came out of his mouth, he could see the fear they produced on her face. "So am I."

11

TRAVELING CIRCUS

Jack pulled over at the general store in the center of town. It was the largest building on the block, and employees were bringing in the miscellaneous items they'd set out for display earlier in the day. As he turned the car off, he watched a family walk down the sidewalk. A young boy tugged at his father's arm. The man had his other arm around his pregnant wife, who smiled and waved at a passing neighbor.

This would have been my hometown. It's like Mayberry. I would have grown up here.

The leather on the steering wheel creaked as Jack's grip tightened. He shut his eyes. He wanted to smash something to keep from feeling anything. He flung open his door and jumped out of the car.

Replacement hurried after him as he marched to the front of the general store. As he pulled the glass door open, a little bell rang overhead. The place was filled with row upon row of neatly stocked shelves and racks of clothes. The checkout was in the back—a throwback to a more innocent age when people were trusted.

Jack spotted a young girl in a red apron stocking some shelves. She stopped as he approached.

"Can I help you?" She was maybe sixteen, with blond pigtails, braces, and a warm smile.

"I need an air mattress."

"We have that." The girl spun around and walked down the aisle. As she searched the shelves, she held her finger out in front of her like a pointer. "Nope... no... it was... here," she proclaimed as she located the one faded box. "Are you using it for sleeping?"

Jack blinked a couple of times and tried not to smirk. "Actually, I'm with a traveling circus and we need it because our net broke."

The girl's eyes became saucers. "Really?"

Jacked laughed. The girl kept smiling, waiting for him to elaborate.

He laughed again, louder. "I'm sorry. I just—"

From down the aisle, there was a loud pop followed by the tinkle of broken glass. The girl jumped, and they both turned to see the source of the commotion.

An old woman stood there, staring at Jack, frozen in place. Her hands were out in front of her. Whatever she'd been holding now lay in a million pieces on the floor. Jack couldn't place the emotions that raced across her face. *Fear. Confusion. Warmth.*

"Are you okay?" Jack walked up to the woman. "You should back up a little way from the glass."

The woman grew paler. One trembling, gnarled hand reached up to her mouth, while the other cinched her jacket tighter to her chest. She stepped forward, her feet crunching the glass.

Jack angled his head and tried to smile as he reached out to steady her. She didn't take his outstretched hand. Instead, she moved closer and touched the side of his face. She must have been in her seventies. She was very small and slightly hunched over. Her white hair was short and wispy, but her blue eyes were bright and now glistened with tears.

"Do I know your parents?" Her voice was a whisper.

Jack swallowed. He opened his mouth and closed it again.

"Mrs. Ritter? Mrs. Ritter!" An older man with a red apron rushed down the aisle toward them.

The woman didn't take her eyes from Jack's face. She smiled at him, and a tear ran down her wrinkled cheek.

Jack stepped back. "I'm not from around here."

The old woman's lip trembled, and her hand fell back to her side.

"I'm sorry, sir," the clerk said. He put his arm around the woman's shoulders.

Jack grabbed the mattress box and bolted for the checkout. As he stormed past, Replacement reached for his arm, but he didn't slow down. He marched to the checkout counter and quickly counted out the bills.

"Jack…"

"Don't. I can't…" He glanced over his shoulder and then shook his head. "Not right now."

Jack kept his eyes on the floor as they retreated to the car. Replacement's door had barely closed when Jack whipped the Impala out of the space. His face was white and his jaw was set.

"Jack…"

"Don't."

"She's your grandmother."

"You don't know that." He smacked the steering wheel. "My mother was a prostitute. How do I know that Steven Ritter even was my father?"

"Jack. Come on."

Jack glared straight ahead and just drove. He wanted to put as much distance between him and the store as quickly as possible.

Replacement put her feet flat on the floor, closed her eyes, and whispered, "Jack, you know he's your fa—"

"I *don't* know. I doubt Patty knew who the real father was. He could have been a hundred different guys."

"Look at that picture! He looks just like you." She scanned his face, confusion evident on her own. "Why are you running away?"

Jack's teeth ground together. "Even if he was, so what? He was probably as crazy as her. He dated a whore. What kind of man—"

"He was seventeen." Replacement cut him off. "Maybe he was nice." She looked down at her hands. "Maybe he was like you."

"Like me?" Jack scoffed. "You don't know him. You don't know me."

He stepped on the gas, and the Impala raced forward.

"I know you." She spun on the seat to stare at him.

"No, you don't." He slammed on the brakes at a red light. "Be glad you don't."

"I do know you. Michelle talked about you all the time."

"That's different. That's the outside. She told you about what I was doing, or stuff we did when we were little. She didn't tell you about *me*." He pointed at his head. "Stuff in here."

Replacement's voice lowered. "She told me about here." She pointed to his heart.

"She wouldn't have told you. Not about… personal things." Jack froze. He stared at the dashboard, and the hairs on the back of his neck rose with his breathing.

"She was worried about you," Replacement whispered.

"Did she…? Damn it," he snarled.

"We were like sisters." Replacement pulled her legs up and hugged them.

Jack's anger swirled the silence into an uncomfortable void between them. "That's a reason for her to break my confidence? What did…?" His mind raced. He had confided everything about himself to Michelle. She was two years younger than he was, but ever since they were kids, she'd been his confidante and advisor.

"After Chandler died… you didn't come back, and she didn't know what was going on with you. Michelle was hurting too, and I think talking about you helped her. She was worried. So… we talked."

I told Michelle everything. All of it. Did she tell Replacement… everything?

The light turned green, and Jack stomped on the accelerator. The Impala's rear tires spun for a second before the car shot forward. Jack snarled. "That doesn't mean you know me."

Replacement looked out the window. When she spoke, her voice was flat. "You know *nothing* about me, Jack."

The realization that she was right hit him in the throat. He caught his breath, and his foot eased off the gas.

Aunt Haddie brought her home when she was, like, eleven. Her real name is Alice, but she doesn't like it. Why? What happened to her parents? The list of unanswered questions was long. Jack glanced over at her, and saw her pensively looking out the window. *Is she thinking about the same things? Her parents? Her past?* She refused to look in his direction, and he couldn't blame her.

She's right. Ever since she showed up in my living room, what have I learned about her? She saved my life, and I treat her like everyone else. I keep her out. I don't want her to know about me, and I don't know anything about her. I take her into my life, but I keep her at a distance. Jack, you're a piece of work.

"I'm sorry." His words hung in the air, but she didn't turn her head. "You're right. I don't know anything about you either."

He heard her exhale, and she put her feet on the floor. Her voice was soft but clear. "I think you're wrong, Jack. Steven Ritter was your father."

Jack pulled over and shut the car off, but he kept looking straight ahead. "I know," he said. "I knew it when I saw the photo. As long as I can remember, I've always wondered who my father was. I'd be somewhere, see some man who looks sort of like me, and think maybe he's my dad… It drove me crazy, but I couldn't stop doing it. I mean, I'd be arresting some guy, and I'd be thinking: Could this be my father?"

Jack ran his hands through his hair. "Now I find him and… I want to deny it. I want to say it's not him. It's some other guy, but not him. That's why I couldn't say anything to Mrs. Ritter. I'd be admitting what I know. Steven Ritter was my father.

And he's dead." Jack leaned his head back. "I just didn't want it to be him. How's that for crazy?"

Rain began to fall. Big wet drops smacked against the windshield and dinged off the roof.

"Jack, that's not crazy—it's normal."

"Crazy is the new black?"

"No. But anyone can understand why you wouldn't want it to be him." Replacement's voice was as soft as a cloud. "I'm sorry your dad is gone."

"Me too."

12

MY TURN

The rain soon turned into a downpour. The gray cloud cover changed to black. The parking lot was a short walk from the inn, so they had to run through the downpour, and they were both soaked by the time they reached the porch at the top of the stairs. The cold rain seemed to invigorate Replacement, and she grinned broadly. It had the opposite effect on Jack. The chill felt as if it sucked the warmth and strength right out of him. He leaned against the wall beside the front doors.

"I'll be one second." He pulled out his cell phone.

"I'll wait." Replacement leaned against the wall next to him.

"You're soaked. Why don't you run up and take a bath?"

Replacement grabbed his jacket and pulled his face closer to hers. "Sweet! Do you know how good that will feel?" Her whole body vibrated.

"Go. Enjoy yourself," Jack said.

She hummed a little tune and happily rushed off upstairs. Jack smiled, but a cold gust of wind and an icy spray of rain quickly extinguished any of the joy he felt at seeing Replacement's enthusiasm. He turned to the wall, pulled out his phone and called Cindy.

"Hello, Cindy Grant speaking."

"Hey, Cindy, it's me, Jack. I need to ask a huge favor."

There was a long pause, and then Cindy cleared her throat.

Jack rolled his eyes and began again. "How are you, Cindy?"

"I'm fine, Jack. Thank you so much for asking. How can I help?"

Jack ran his fingers through his dripping-wet hair. "I need you to run some background checks."

Jack gave her all the information he had on the three men named Terry.

"Got it." Jack could hear Cindy's pen scratching. "How should I get it to you? Do you have email out in the sticks?"

"Yeah. I have my smartphone." Jack leaned closer to the wall and tucked his head down into his jacket. "And can you run one more? Alice Campbell."

"Alice? Our Alice?"

"Yes, Cindy, please?"

There was another long pause. "Jack, are you all right?"

The rough wooden shingles dug into the back of Jack's hand as he pushed against the wall. "I'm good, Cindy. Thanks. I appreciate this." And he hung up.

The rain was torrential now, but it made everything around Jack sparkle. The lights from the inn reflected off the drops shattering against the porch. Jack could picture the old woman's face. He could still hear the breaking bowl and the glass chiming as it bounced along the floor.

She knew. I'm his son. My father was murdered. I had no control over that.

Jack stepped out from under the eave of the shallow porch and turned his face upward. The rain ran down his cheeks. He opened his eyes and stared into the blackness.

I control the here and now. And now—it's my turn.

13

TEA AND A BATH

Inside the inn, Jack stopped. Water practically poured off of him, leaving a puddle on the cranberry-red welcome mat.

"Mr. Stratton?" Ms. Jenkins called from behind the front counter. "Mr. Stratton, you're dripping on my floor."

Jack met her disapproving gaze. She raised one eyebrow and folded her hands in front of her. She wore a light-brown period dress, but instead of a traditional high neckline, this one was cut low. She reached behind the counter, grabbed two towels, and hurried over to the door.

"Thank you." Jack took both towels and squatted down to wipe the floor. "My apologies."

"I can do that, Mr. Stratton." She tried to take back one of the towels, but Jack was already mopping up the puddle.

"I made the mess, I can clean it up. You can call me Jack." He stood up and handed her the wet towel. The warmth of her fingers on his cold skin sent a glow racing down his wrist.

She inhaled sharply, then slowly exhaled. The faint smell of chamomile reached him, and he grinned roguishly. Her eyes connected with his. "Can I get you anything else, Mr. Stratton?" The muscles around her eyes and mouth twitched slightly, revealing her struggle to keep a mask of refinement on her face.

Jack wiped the back of his neck with the other towel and waited a moment before answering. "I've had a rough day," he said. "Do you have anything to drink?"

Her expression soured. "Mr. Stratton, there's a bar downtown—"

Jack leaned back and feigned a look of shock. His mind raced. "Ms. Jenkins, on a cold night like this, I was... only thinking of having a cup of tea to warm me."

She looked at him incredulously. "Tea? *You* wanted a cup of tea?"

Save. "I got caught in that downpour. Now I'm chilled to the bone. I thought I might go back to my room, get a good book, and relax in the bath with a nice cup of tea."

Her mouth dropped open.

Jack looked at her as innocently as a child. He was laying it on thick. Her head tilted slightly to the side, and her pursed lips relaxed and then slowly opened. Jack resisted the urge to smile as her eyes traveled over him. She appeared to be revising her opinion of him.

Jack handed her the other towel. "Well, I guess I'll have to remember to pick some up in town next time. I'm sorry to have troubled you, Ms. Jenkins."

Slump your shoulders. Small smile. Nod. Jack moved slowly toward the staircase.

"Mr. Stratton, is there a particular brand of tea you prefer?"

Jack had one foot on the stairs. He turned around.

Ms. Jenkins walked forward, and her hands were now behind her back.

"Well," he said, "it sounds a little silly, but on a rainy night like this, I just love a cup of chamomile tea."

The woman's eyebrows lifted and her chest heaved.

Bang. Set the hook. Jack Stratton, you are so bad.

They both moved closer, and Jack could once again smell the flowers on her breath.

"Would you like me to bring some up?" she offered.

He gently touched her arm, nodded his head—then clamped his mouth shut when he remembered: *Replacement's upstairs. Damn.*

"What's wrong?"

"My…" Jack coughed. "Coworker."

"That young woman isn't your girlfriend?" Disbelief and surprise, followed by understanding, flashed across the woman's face.

Jack shrugged and nodded.

"That's why you wanted another room."

Game over. I shouldn't be flirting anyway. "Thanks anyhow." He sighed. Jack turned and started back up.

"Can I at least get you a cup to take back to your room?" she asked with a smile that begged him to follow her. She never took her eyes off him as she backed toward the open door behind the counter.

Jack swallowed and forced himself to walk slowly after her. Her hand traced along the wood of the countertop. She was using it to guide herself as she walked backward, but the soft, feminine gesture sent a spark up Jack's spine.

Smiling, she turned and walked into the back room. It was a dark interior room with only two tall lamp stands for light. "I'll be right back. The water's already hot," she said. She disappeared through another door.

Jack scanned the room. All the furniture was antique, as was the rug, and he was still soaking wet. He debated running upstairs and changing, but quickly drove that thought from his mind. He took one look at the well-preserved chairs and couch and chose to remain standing, slowly dripping on the carpet. He shivered, and the cold rushed back into his being. His head fell forward; he leaned against the doorjamb and closed his eyes. The smell of the old house mixed with the scent of the rain was calming. He inhaled a couple of times and cleared his throat.

His eyes opened at the sound of the other door clicking shut. Ms. Jenkins stood in the doorway with a tea tray in her left hand and a robe over her right arm. Her eyes met his, and warmth spread inside his chest. Jack grinned and strode forward. He could see the flush on her neck as she swallowed.

"I thought you might need to warm up. I can dry your clothes." She set the tray on a small table beside the couch and walked over to him, both arms held out with the robe draped over them. "You can use that room to change." She tilted her head toward a small door, but didn't take her eyes off Jack.

"Thank you." He took the robe and headed for the room she'd indicated. *Slow down. Cool. Think about what you're doing…* It was a small bathroom with just a sink, a toilet, and an ornate, full-length mirror stand. Jack's hands shook as he removed his clothes. He couldn't tell whether it was from the cold or nervousness.

How old is she? Mid-forties? She doesn't look it. Dancer? Guaranteed she's a dancer.

The robe could have been custom-made for him. It was dark-blue with an ornate trim, matching the historical feel of the house, and it was soft and warm, as if she'd just taken it out of the dryer. Jack relaxed into the warmth and closed his eyes. When he reopened them, he straightened up, checked himself in the mirror, and stood even taller. The robe gave him a regal appearance. He spoke into the mirror. "Lord Jack of Tingsberry."

He opened the door. The woman was seated at the end of the couch.

Jack paused.

She smiled and held out a cup. "Tea?"

Jack sat down at the other end of the couch and took the ornate teacup with a widening smile. "Thank you..." He let his words hang in the air—he realized he didn't know her name.

"Kristine," she answered with a slight nod.

A small moan escaped Jack's lips as he sipped the tea. "That's really good tea," he said, surprised. He wasn't a tea man at all.

Kristine smiled broadly, set her cup down, and folded her hands in her lap. "Tea and a bath..." She tilted her head. "Do you really like to take baths?"

Jack thought about continuing the charade, but one look at her face caused him to dismiss the idea.

She's smart. She'll see right through it.

"You're right. I haven't taken a bath since I was seven." He smiled.

"Which probably wasn't that long ago."

Jack saw his chance for romance plummeting. In situations like this, he went to his old standby: he told the truth.

"Kristine, I wasn't interested in a bath or tea. Honestly, at first I wanted to tease you a little for not giving me a room refund, but..." He exhaled and looked into her eyes. "There was also something about you. The way you move, like a dancer. When I got close to you, I could feel your breath and I smelled the chamomile."

"I *thought* that part was too good to be true. You're a good detective. What do you do for a living?"

Jack lifted his chin. "I'm a cop."

"Figures." She leaned in. "I *was* a dancer."

Jack leaned in, but he was still taken aback when in one swift move she kissed him. *Think about what you're doing. I shouldn't. I shouldn't... I should.*

With one hand, Jack lifted her up slightly off the couch and pulled her forward enough to be reclining. The move was so fast and fluid that Kristine exhaled as he gently laid her down. Jack's eyes closed as he let the different sensations wash over him: the softness of her hair in his left hand, the firmness of her toned back in his right. Chamomile danced faintly on his tongue. Her hands drew him closer, and his leg rubbed against hers.

"That was some kiss," she whispered.

He opened his eyes and smiled as she searched his face. Long lashes led to blue eyes that widened.

But then Kristine's face went white. She pressed her lips together and her body went rigid. "Get out."

Jack froze. "I'm sorry. Did I..."

"Just leave, please."

This was the age of "no means no," but he couldn't understand the one-eighty turnaround. "Are you all right?"

"*Now.*" She clenched her jaw and turned her head toward the back of the couch.

Jack carefully lifted himself off her and backed up toward the door. He moved quietly and quickly but hesitated when he grabbed the old doorknob.

"I'm sorry if..." He trailed off.

Kristine pulled her legs up and curled into a ball. He opened the door just enough to slip through, then closed it behind him.

Damn it! My clothes.

Jack stood behind the desk in the ornate robe. His shoes, pants, and, most importantly, his keys were in the bathroom. He debated with himself for only a moment, then headed up the stairs.

This blows. This is so bad.

He pulled the robe tighter around himself as the young couple from yesterday's breakfast walked past him. They gave him an odd look, and he could hear them giggle.

Damn.

14

COMPLIMENTARY LAUNDRY

Jack sheepishly walked up to the room and knocked.

Replacement opened the door. "What happened to you?" She snickered as he walked into the room. "Where did you get that robe?"

"Um... my clothes were wet. The... front desk offered... to do the complimentary laundry."

"They do laundry?" Her neck lengthened, and her nose crinkled.

"Yeah. So they gave me a robe." Jack cringed at his lie.

"Can they dry my stuff?"

"No, they... only do one load per room a day. I'm sorry."

"It's okay." Her shoulders popped up and down. "I hung mine up in the bathroom. Do you want to take a bath?"

"No." Jack shook his head rapidly.

"Are you going to sleep with me tonight?" Replacement asked innocently.

Jack's head snapped up at the question, and his neck flushed. Replacement's expression didn't change. Jack sighed. "No. Thank you."

"Please sleep with me." She put her hands together in a mock begging position.

Jack swallowed. "I have... my air mattress." He grabbed the box and held it up, turning away quickly.

"Suit yourself." Replacement climbed back on the bed.

Jack pulled out the air mattress and started to blow it up. But after several minutes of huffing and puffing, the mattress was still only half-filled. Jack leaned back against the bureau, and Replacement slid off the bed.

"Want some help?" She picked up the corner of the mattress and began to blow air into it. After only a few breaths, she hit his leg. "See? I'm so much better at this than you. It's almost all the way up." She inhaled deeply and blew into the valve again.

"Okay. That's good enough."

Replacement stopped, put down the mattress, and leaned onto it. It made a creaking sound as she bounced.

"I can sleep here," she offered. "This is bouncy."

"No. That's good. Thank you. I'll sleep here."

"Suit yourself. But how about right now, you get some real clothes on. I want to go down to dinner. I'm starving!"

"Again? Are you ever *not* starving?"

Replacement patted her stomach and smiled. "What can I say? Undercover work makes me hungry."

Jack rolled his eyes.

* * *

Jack forced himself to remain absolutely motionless on the air mattress. The slightest movement would cause the whole bed to wobble like Jell-O.

Make a list for tomorrow. Get the info from Cindy. One by one, talk to the three suspects. What the hell happened with Kristine? Did she… maybe she just changed her mind. I didn't see a ring. No indentation. What about…?

Jack gradually became aware of a slight hissing sound coming from the mattress. He shifted his position, and it changed to a noise like a kid's whoopee cushion. Jack froze, and the noise stopped. But a moment later he moved his head—and that was enough to cause another noise. It sounded like someone farted, and it lasted for a few seconds this time.

Damn it.

Jack waited until the sound stopped. He listened for several more moments, then rolled his head back to look up at the ceiling.

Suddenly the mattress busted out into a long and loud farting noise—the sound of someone who had eaten way too much fiber. And this time it kept going. Replacement giggled, and Jack couldn't help himself: he did, too. Soon they were both crying with laughter as his bed deflated.

Jack's body finally settled onto the hard floor, and the laughter stopped. He wrapped his blanket tightly around himself as he lay on his back and stared at the ceiling.

But despite how tired he was, sleep wouldn't come. Every time he shut his eyes, he could see his mother's face. It would change back and forth between her young self and the woman at the institution. In his mind she was silently screaming, her finger outstretched, terror in her eyes.

And now three more faces tormented him. There was the old woman from the store, the tears rolling down her cheeks and her trembling lips. And there was his father, though his face was unclear. Jack could bring it up in his mind, but it lacked detail. And finally, there was Kristine. For some reason her face haunted him too.

Why did she freak out?

Just outside the door, Jack heard the floor creak. Jack silently drew his legs up, rolled over, and crouched. He hadn't heard the footsteps approach, but he did hear them leaving. His hand hesitated on the doorknob before he cracked the door open.

Next to the door were his clothes, neatly folded in a pile, with his shoes on top. Jack quietly picked them up and retreated into the room.

15

THE FOREMAN

The next morning after breakfast, Jack sat in their room, reading over the reports Cindy had sent him, while Replacement showered. It was annoying reading on a tiny phone; Jack much preferred paper.

Replacement came out of the bathroom wearing her new "I Love Hope Falls" shirt and hat. She stopped short. "You gonna shower? You look like crap."

"Gee, thanks." He looked into the mirror in the bathroom, and he had to admit that Replacement was right: he looked like hell. His skin was pale and there were dark circles under his eyes. Even his pupils seemed black. "C'mon, let's go."

Jack wanted to get moving. He didn't want to hang around the inn any longer than he had to—and risk running into Kristine. All through breakfast he had worried she'd show up, but she never did. Maybe she was hiding from him too. He hoped so.

He hurried out of the room. Replacement chased after him.

"What's the first stop?" She had to jog to stay beside him.

"Terry Bradford. He's a foreman at K and K Construction. It's a ten-minute drive."

"How did you find that out?"

"Cindy got me his information. Guy has bounced from one low-level job to another. One DUI. Married three times. Divorced. Four kids by three different mothers. Two bankruptcies."

"Boy, he's a keeper. Do you want me to drive?"

Jack shot her a crooked frown, so when they got out to the car, she headed for the passenger side.

"Do you have a plan?" she asked hopefully.

Jack jumped in the car quickly, still worrying about being seen by Kristine. He started the engine and sped out of the little parking lot. "It's 9:04. Construction workers should all be there by now."

"Okay... but do you have a plan?"

"No. I'll play it by ear."

Replacement raised her eyebrows. "Well... shouldn't we come up with a plan first?"

"Okay, here's the plan. Don't scream, and don't yell, as I calmly ask him if he had anything to do with murdering my father. And if he gives me a sideways glance, I'm going to beat him to death."

"That sounds like a great plan." Replacement's lip curled.

Jack punched it.

As they headed through downtown, Jack noticed an old white pickup weaving through traffic behind them. He pulled down the rearview mirror and slowed down.

"Is everything okay?" Replacement craned her neck to look behind them.

The pickup took a sharp right from the left lane, then disappeared from view behind a building.

"I'm just paranoid." Jack positioned the rearview mirror back.

The Impala slid into the parking lot at K and K Construction. The mini-mountains of gravel, sand, and stone behind the structure dwarfed the building. Giant machines loaded trucks while a group of men gathered out front. A couple of the men stopped and turned toward Jack as he walked up to them.

"I'm looking for Terry Bradford," Jack said.

The men just glanced at each other and then back at Jack.

"Just point me in the right direction," Jack grumbled.

They looked at each other again. As a cop, Jack had seen the look a thousand times. *No one wants to be a snitch.*

Replacement tapped Jack's shoulder and tilted her head toward the building. A group of five men in green shirts, jeans, and work boots were marching out of the office. Jack zeroed in on the guy in the middle.

Early forties. Five ten. Two hundred pounds.

Terry Bradford was twenty-six years older than the yearbook photo and had apparently shaved his head now, but Jack knew it was him.

Jack jogged over. "Terry, you got a second?"

Four of the men stopped. Terry kept walking.

"I just have a few questions." Jack forced a smile onto his face.

"I'm workin'. Talk to me later." Terry held up a hand.

"It'll only take a second." Jack stepped in front of him. "I need to ask you about Steven Ritter."

"Who? I don't know any Ritter. Get the hell out of my way, or I'll break your nose." Terry stopped and made a face as if he had drunk extra-sour lemonade.

"Steven Ritter. You went to high school with him."

"Ritter? Was that the kid who got killed at the pond?"

"Yes."

"I didn't know him. He was a year under me. He didn't play football, right?" Jack shook his head.

"Then I didn't know him. We gotta be someplace," Terry snapped. He stepped forward and got right in Jack's face. "Move."

Nose to nose, they glared at each other. "Did you know Patricia Cole?" Jack asked calmly.

Terry made a face again. "Patty? Put-out Patty?" His tongue hung out of his open mouth as he laughed. "Everyone knew Patty... if you know what I mean."

Jack's hand twitched into a fist, and Replacement put her hand on his arm.

"You guys on vacation?" a large man bellowed from the building's doorway. "Get your asses in gear, now!"

Replacement kept her hand on Jack's arm while Terry walked around him and climbed behind the wheel of the truck. The veins in Jack's neck stood out.

"Not now," she whispered. "Get him alone."

As the truck pulled out of the parking lot, Terry roared with laughter and pounded the side of the door. Jack turned and stormed back to the Impala. Replacement dashed over to it and stood in front of his door.

"Out of my way," Jack said.

"Not now, Jack." She put both hands on the door handle. "You taught me that. Wait until you can ask him alone. You know where he lives, right?"

"He could be the guy who killed my father."

"He could, or he might not be."

Jack glared at the sky. *Damn it. I'm too close to this. I can't think straight.* He looked down at Replacement and nodded.

"We'll go and talk to him tonight," Replacement said. "When he's alone."

"I'll get him to talk to me then."

Replacement didn't move.

"You gonna let me get in my car?" Jack asked.

Replacement ignored the question. "Jack, what are you doing? You went straight at Terry. We can't do that with this next guy. You know what to do. What questions to ask. You're a policeman."

"Not out here I'm not. Not right now."

Replacement squared her shoulders. "Yes, right now." She pointed at his heart. "You're always a cop." Then she tapped her temple. "But you need to be one here too. After all, when we do find the guy, and we will, we need to get evidence that we can take to the police, not kill the guy."

She smiled.

Jack didn't.

"We *are* going to take the evidence to the police, right?"

Jack didn't answer her. He gently pushed her aside and opened his door. "Let's go talk to Terry Martin."

16

THE FIDUCIARY

Jack scanned the large brass mailbox next to the entrance of the office building. A number of names were etched into the plates. "Two oh six. Second floor," he snapped as he held open the door.

Replacement looked up at him and flashed a big smile. "How about letting me do the talking on this one?"

"I said keep me in check, not on a leash. I'll do the talking. Just make sure I don't flip out."

"How am I going to do that? Can I have a gun?"

"No." He winced. "Is that your plan? Shoot me?"

"I wasn't thinking that, but since you suggested it…" Her hands went out, and she grinned impishly. "I just don't want *you* shooting anyone."

"I'm not going to shoot anyone. I wouldn't use a gun to kill him, anyway."

"That's reassuring."

As they walked inside, the polished marble floor shined in the sunlight. The fixtures were gleaming metal with glass accents. This place was clearly upscale.

"The tenants must pay a lot for rent here," Replacement noted.

As they headed for the staircase, Jack went cold thinking about what he would do when he did find the guy who killed his father. He forced the thought away. That wasn't something to dwell on—yet.

They wound their way through the second floor until they found office 206. Jack stopped before a large oak door with a bronze sign that read: *Terry Martin—Fiduciary Advisor.*

Jack pointed at the sign. "This is the one who looked like a weasel," he spat.

"That might not be the best way to start."

Jack opened the door into what appeared to be the receptionist's office. An elegant oak desk sat across from them, with a closed oak door to one side and four leather chairs to the other. A glass coffee table with a neat stack of magazines was just in front of them, and beside the chairs was another little table with yet more magazines, artfully arranged. But the office was empty.

Jack and Replacement exchanged a shrug as they walked in. Jack moved over behind the desk. The computer was on, and there was a cup of coffee next to the keyboard.

Replacement cleared her throat and tilted her head toward the closed door. She raised her eyebrows twice. Jack listened carefully, and then he understood Replacement's reaction. From behind the door came the sounds of lovemaking.

Replacement made a disgusted face. "Maybe we should go," she whispered.

Jack rapped hard on the door.

"Or not." Replacement stepped back.

A minute later, the door opened and a young, disheveled, blond secretary stood wide-eyed before them, smiling awkwardly.

"Who is it?" a man's voice called out from behind her.

Jack walked right past her and through the door.

A tall, middle-aged man adjusted his clothes as he moved behind his desk. Terry Martin had a large nose, a pockmarked face, and dyed hair that he combed over.

"Do you have an appointment?" he snapped as he sat down, still adjusting his clothes.

"My name is Jack Stratton." Jack strode over to the two chairs in front of the desk and sat down. He didn't offer the man his hand. "I have a few questions for you."

"Are you looking for financial advice?"

"Did you know Patricia Cole?" Jack asked.

"Subtle," Replacement whispered as she slid into the seat next to him.

"What?" Terry swiveled in his high-back chair. "Cole? I knew a Patty Cole, but that was in high school."

"How did you know Patty?"

"What? Who are you?"

"Did you know Patty? Did you date her?"

"Date her? You didn't 'date' Patty. We, uh… I was—Did my wife send you?" Terry leaned forward. "That hag. She can't get anything on me, so she goes back to some slut I screwed in high school?"

Jack's knuckles went white on the chair. The muscles in his jaw flexed, and Replacement shifted in her seat. Terry jumped up, and so did Replacement.

She held up her hands. "We don't know your wife. We're doing some historical research and we're hoping you could please—"

Terry stormed around the desk, grabbed her by the arm, and yanked her toward the door. "Get the hell out—"

"Let go of her." Jack flew out of his chair.

Terry let go, stumbled backward, and fell. He banged into the wall on the way down, and a picture crashed to the floor, its glass cracking.

"You piece of garbage." Jack stepped toward him menacingly.

"Jack!" Replacement held Jack's arm.

"Terry!" The office door flew open, and the secretary hurried in. "Leave him alone!"

She rushed toward Jack, but Replacement stepped between them, her feet wide and her shoulders square.

"Your boyfriend fell," Replacement said.

"What about Steven? Steven Ritter?" Jack towered over Terry.

"Steve?" Terry didn't even try to get up. "The kid who was murdered at the pond?"

"Did you know him?"

"He was in some of my classes. I knew him since we were kids. Why? What does this have to do with my wife?"

"I don't know your wife. Get up."

Terry froze. "I don't know anything about Steven getting killed. Did someone say I did? That's crazy."

"I'm calling the police," the secretary said.

Replacement shook her head. "There's no need for that. We were just leaving."

"You knew Steven," Jack said. He was still glaring at Terry. "I said get up."

Terry rose, but he kept his hands out in front of himself like he was facing a wild dog. "I liked Steve. I had nothing to do with it. I couldn't stab someone. I've never even been in a fight. I can't fight my way out of a paper bag. Honest. I don't know why anyone would say... Wait. Was it Patty? Is she still mad at me? If Patty said I had anything to do with it, she's just out for revenge."

"Revenge for what?" Jack asked.

"She—she wanted to join the band. I told her I could get her in. It was just a con. I really just wanted to get in her pants. But that was a long time ago."

"You used her." Jack took a step forward. The broken glass on the floor crunched beneath his heel.

"I was in high school! Guys did that crap."

"Looks like you haven't learned your lesson." Replacement tilted her head toward the secretary, who was now fuming.

Terry scurried behind his desk. "I'm calling the police." He reached for the phone.

Replacement jerked her thumb at the secretary, whose disgusted glare was withering. "Right now, Terry, I'd be more worried that *she's* going to call your *wife*."

Terry straightened up and combed back his hair. "Get out. Now."

Jack spoke in a low voice. "Here's the deal. I don't care who the hell you call. I want to know where you were the night Steven was killed." He put his hand on the desk.

Terry's eyes widened. "Wait a second... Are you... You're Steven's son."

Jack walked around the desk, his fists clenched.

"Wait! I can prove I had nothing to do with it. I was in *Spain*!" He shouted the word. "The whole AP Spanish class went. I had to call my mom to find out who got killed. The teacher only told us someone from school died. There's got to be a record of the trip and who was on it."

Jack's head pounded. He glared at Terry, who took another step back.

"I liked Steven. I did. Check. Check with the school."

"I will."

Jack spun on his heel and headed for the door.

As he and Replacement stormed out of the office, they heard the secretary's voice behind them. "Helping me get by the CPA exam—was that just a lie to get in my pants, too?"

* * *

Jack's anger boiled over. Getting to the car and leaving was a blur. He had no clue where he was going; he was just driving.

"Jack? Jack, pull over," Replacement urged. Jack kept driving. "Pull over." Replacement put her hand on the door handle, like she was about to open it. "Now."

Jack knew she was serious. He hit the brake and pulled over.

"Jack..."

He threw the door open and jumped out of the car. She did, too.

"What the hell were you thinking, Jack?"

"What was I thinking?" Jack spun around. "I wasn't thinking at all." He could see the shock on her face. He could only imagine how *he* looked. "I wanted to beat him to death. I didn't just want to hurt him; I wanted him *dead*. Okay? Is that what you want to hear? I'm not thinking straight." Jack's eyes were black, and his hands shook.

"Jack, I don't think he had anything to do with it."

"I don't either, but right now I don't care." He kicked a rock off the road and into the woods. "I just... Damn it! It's not just Steven. It's Patty too. I don't know why, but I keep thinking of Patty as a kid. She just wanted to get into the band, and he used her. I should have done something."

Replacement crossed her arms over her chest. "Maybe we should go back home. Just for a while. You're losing all perspective."

"I'm not going anywhere," Jack growled. "Someone killed my father. I have to find out who." He glared up at the gray sky and wanted to scream.

"Jack, you're going to do something you're seriously going to regret if you don't keep your anger in check."

"We still have to go talk to the other Terry," Jack said.

"What?" Replacement threw her hands up. "You just... Do you think talking to the other guy is at all wise after what you just did? So far, your plan is to yell and accuse. You're not even asking questions. That last guy has an alibi—a good one—and we can check it out. But you're just screaming. That's just stupid."

"*One* of them did it. I just need to figure out which one."

"No. Not with me you're not. I'm having nothing more to do with your professional suicide."

Jack looked down at his hands. His head pounded. "Fine. I'll let you do the talking this time."

Replacement didn't move.

He hung his head and tried to slow his breathing. "Please?"

Replacement put her hands on her hips and shook her head. She searched his eyes, and then exhaled. "I'll do it, but you have to agree to three things. First, I do all the talking." She held up a hand. "*All* the talking."

"Fine."

"Second, I drive." She held out a hand, and he tossed her the keys.

"Third, you sleep in the stupid bed tonight."

Jack hesitated, but then said, "Agreed."

Replacement's face softened. "Jack, I'm worried about you."

"Don't be." Jack walked to the passenger side. "After all, I've got you watching my back. What could go wrong?"

17

NOTHING TO WORRY ABOUT

Jack glanced at the side-view mirror. A police car was driving behind them. "Cop," he muttered.

"I see him." Replacement held her hands at a perfect ten and two position on the steering wheel. She stopped at the stop sign and put her blinker on. "We have nothing to worry about as long as we obey the speed limits, and since I'm driving—"

Blue lights flashed and a siren kicked on.

"You were saying?" Jack said.

"What the heck?" Replacement pulled over. "I didn't do anything wrong."

"I bet Terry Martin called the cops." Jack sat up straighter. "I knew I should have put him through the wall."

"That would have been a big help." Replacement made a face as she got her license out.

A policeman with a crisp white shirt and salt-and-pepper hair marched over to Replacement's window. "License and registration."

She handed him her license and registration. "What seems to be the problem, officer?" she asked innocently.

The policeman took the paperwork and headed back to the cruiser without saying a word.

"That was rude," Replacement muttered.

"He's a lieutenant." Jack watched him in the side-view mirror. "The town's so small they must have everyone pulling patrol."

"But I didn't do anything. Do you really think Terry called?"

Jack shook his head. "No. He didn't ask for my license or even look at me."

They waited in silence for a while. At last the policeman came back and handed Replacement a ticket.

"What?" Her voice went high as she read the ticket. "Failure to yield at an intersection?"

"She came to a full stop," Jack protested.

"You can contest it." The policeman's voice was flat.

One look at the man's set jaw and unsympathetic expression, and Jack knew that arguing was most likely pointless. But he still had to try. He leaned over and read the man's nametag. "Lieutenant Nelson, sir, I can assure you that she did come to a complete—"

"You can explain it at traffic court." Nelson straightened up and folded his hands in front of himself. "Your girlfriend needs to obey the law. Have a nice day." He started back for his car.

Jack bristled. "What a jerk."

Replacement started the Impala.

The flashing blue lights shut off behind them, and Jack tried, unsuccessfully, not to glare as Nelson pulled out and drove away.

"Maybe we should just go back to the hotel," Replacement suggested.

"No. I agreed to your terms. We go talk to Terry Martinez first."

18

THE ART TEACHER

Terry Martinez's house was a modest Cape Cod, painted a deep-red with black shutters. It fit right in with the other four beautiful homes on the cul-de-sac. A group of children rode bikes down the sidewalk, and a cinnamon-brown sedan was parked in the driveway.

"Okay," Replacement said. "Terry Martinez. He's a teacher?"

"High school art. Widower. Wife died five years ago. No arrests. Finances in order."

"I do all the talking, right?"

Jack moved his fingers in a horizontal zipping motion across his mouth.

Just as they got out of the car, a middle-aged man opened the front door and stepped outside. His black hair was tinted gray at the sides. He was short and his blue T-shirt revealed a bit of a paunch. He tipped his head to the side, stopped halfway down the steps, and waited for them to approach.

"Terry Martinez?" Replacement smiled as she held out her hand. "I'm Alice Campbell. This is Jack Stratton."

Replacement's nose crinkled as she said her own name, but it was the look Terry gave Jack that caught Jack's attention. Terry's eyes moved to look at Jack's mouth, nose, chin, and finally his eyes. Jack held out his hand, and Terry hesitated before shaking it firmly.

"How can I help you?" Terry's mouth curled up at the corner.

"I was wondering if we could speak with you about some people you went to high school with," Replacement said.

"High school." He smiled and adjusted his glasses. "That was a long time ago, but I'd be happy to. Uh… do you want to come in?"

"That's very kind of you."

They followed Terry into the house. It was not at all what Jack had expected from an art teacher's home. It was a very neat and tidy, conservative house. Terry led them to a traditional living room and motioned them to a small couch.

"Can I get you something to drink?"

"No, thank you," Replacement answered, and Jack shook his head.

Terry sat in a worn but comfortable-looking blue chair. "How can I help you?"

"We were wondering if you knew a Patricia Cole?" Replacement said.

Terry leaned back, frowned, and nodded. "Patty. I knew her. She grew up over on Winston. No brothers or sisters."

"Can you tell us a little about her?"

Terry took off his glasses and cleaned them on his shirt. "What's this all about?"

"We're doing some family research, and it would be very helpful if you could fill in some information we need."

Terry's eyes went wide; he stared at Jack. He tilted his head and pursed his lips. "I never thought... Patty is your mother."

"How did you know?" Jack asked, surprised.

Terry smiled and patted the arm of his chair. "The resemblance. I'm an artist. I've got a thing for faces. I knew you must be Steve's son—"

Replacement gasped.

Terry looked nervously at both of them. "You knew that, right?"

"Yes," Jack said. "And I admit I look a little like him."

"A little? You're not identical, but it's darn close. The whole shape of your face. The eyes are spot on. Indistinguishable." He clucked his tongue and held up a hand. "One second." Terry hurried out of the room and returned a moment later carrying a framed photo. "Here."

Jack took the frame, and Replacement slid closer. Four boys in shorts held up fishing poles, each with a tiny fish at the end. They were all smiling. Steven was in the middle. He must have been in his early teens.

"He looks just like you," Replacement said.

Terry sat back down and sniffed. "I'm so sorry about Steven. You couldn't have known him, right?"

Jack shook his head. "I didn't even know his name before this week."

"Is this you?" Replacement asked Terry, pointing to a fat kid in the photo, with curly black hair and a giant smile.

"Sure is. I was chubbier then."

"Were you friends?" Replacement asked.

"The four of us were best friends. Same Boy Scout troop. We knew each other since preschool."

"Who are the other boys?"

"Trent Dorsey and Dennis Wilson. Trent passed ten years ago. Car accident in Baltimore."

"And Dennis?"

"He's the police chief. He lives on Davidson. Big gray colonial."

Jack held up a hand. "Dennis Wilson? Dennis Wilson was chief when Steven died. How old is he?"

"Oh, that was Dennis Senior. His son became chief maybe twelve years ago."

Steven's friend is now chief. I've a much better shot at the police reports now.

Terry frowned. "Steven was a good guy. I don't know if anyone... Well..." Terry's eyes filled with concern as he looked at Jack. "Steven's mother still lives in town."

Replacement leaned in. "We're going to speak with her later. You knew Patty?"

"I did. It's a small town, so everyone knows everybody. She was in my class in high school."

Replacement's voice softened. "Did you ever... date her?"

"Date? No. I had a huge crush on her in middle school. I wouldn't go near her then because of her father. Mr. Cole's as mean as they come. He's a drinker, too. I thought about it in high school, but she'd gotten a... well." Terry started to clean his glasses again, but this time he didn't look up.

Jack broke the awkward silence. "I've heard. She had a reputation."

Terry exhaled. "In high school, she did. Something changed in her in middle school. It was after her mom died. Maybe it was that. Maybe it was her father. I don't know. She just seemed to fly apart. I didn't know Steven dated her."

"You never knew they dated?" Replacement asked.

"No, but... boy, just thinking about it. On the one hand, it was twenty-something years ago, but on the other it feels like yesterday." Terry smiled sadly. "Steve was getting over a bad breakup shortly before he was killed. I didn't think he'd started dating again." Terry smiled sideways at Jack. "I was always jealous of your dad. Steve was such a good kid. He was such a Boy Scout. I mean, we were all technically Boy Scouts, but he was the real deal—you know what I mean. And back then, with Patty's reputation... Well, Steve wasn't the type of guy to go with..."

Jack finished the sentence. "A girl like that?"

Terry nodded. "I came back for the funeral—"

"Came back?" Jack asked.

"My parents divorced at the start of my senior year. My dad stayed in Hope Falls, but I'd moved to Cincinnati with my mom."

"You weren't living here when he was killed?"

"No. I was living in Ohio then." The teacher's eyes went wide, and he sat back. "Wait a minute. Are you looking into it? Me? Why would you think I had anything to do with it?"

"Settle down." Jack stood. "I don't think you had anything to do with it."

"Good, because I didn't. Steve was my friend."

"I believe you."

"I don't." Replacement said it quietly, but they both heard her.

"What?" Terry held up his hands.

"Well..." She shrugged. "I don't know. You show us a picture and act all nice, but it could be an act."

"Why would you think I had anything to do with it? I wasn't even in the state."

"We got a tip," Jack said.

"A tip to look at *me*?" Terry sat up straight.

"They weren't specific. They only had a first name: Terry." Jack ran his hands through his hair. "Thank you for your time."

"Wait." Terry stood. "There were a couple of other guys named Terry. Terry Martin. He was a pain in the ass at school. Martin and Martinez? People always got us confused. They could have meant him?"

"I talked to him already."

"Did he say anything?" Terry paced. "There was also a Terry in the grade above us. Football player. He was a jerk."

"Talked to him, too. Thank you." Jack headed for the door.

Replacement followed, but she turned at the doorway. "Would it be possible to talk to you again, please?"

"Sure. And Jack, if I said anything to offend you, I'm sorry. If you need anything, please let me help."

* * *

As Jack stomped back to the car, Replacement grabbed his shoulder. "What the hell was that? Why are we leaving?"

"What? I didn't do anything, like I promised. And now you're pissed? I didn't hit him."

"He's the first person who would talk to us. He knew both your parents."

"Don't call them that," Jack snapped.

"He knew them both. He might know something that will help."

"He just gave us an alibi we can check out. We back off for now and let him sweat. Just because his mother moved to Cincinnati doesn't mean he didn't come back to visit his father for a weekend. I plan on talking to him later, but not now. I want to go back to the inn and think."

Replacement shrugged. "I guess you're right. Tonight you can get a good night's sleep, and tomorrow will be a new day, right?"

If I make it to tomorrow.

19

DROWN IT

Jack splashed water on his face and reached for a towel.

Terry. Terry who? Patty gets him killed and she can't even tell me the last name of the guy who killed him?

He looked in the mirror and barely recognized himself: he was pale and gaunt, his brown eyes set deep in his skull.

I have to get some sleep. I look like death.

Jack walked out of the bathroom and stopped in his tracks. Replacement had his phone in her hands and looked as if she wanted to kill him.

"What?"

She held the phone up. "I went to look at the report for Terry Bradford and saw this. You asked Cindy to run a background check on me?"

Jack froze. "No—I—we got in that fight about not knowing each other, so I wanted to find out more about you."

"So you had Cindy run a *background check*?" She was so mad she was practically shaking.

"How else was I going to find out more about you?"

"How about asking! You could have—you should—" Replacement ran into the bathroom and slammed the door.

Damn.

Jack's fist came down on the bureau, and something cracked.

Damn damn damn.

He stormed over to the closet, locked his gun in the safe, grabbed his wallet and keys, and headed out the door. He stomped straight to his car.

Jack drummed his fingers on the steering wheel as he fought to drive out the thoughts that assaulted him. It didn't work. Rage seethed inside him. Pain. Hurt. It was useless to fight it now.

The only way I know to kill the pain… is to drown it.

Jack didn't have to drive far before he found a hole-in-the-wall, single-room bar on a side road. As he entered, he paused for a second to let his eyes adjust to the dim light.

Then he smiled.

My kind of bar.

A man in his sixties with pale skin, yellowed teeth, and dull black eyes stood behind the bar. Of the seven guys in the room, three looked at Jack, but only for a moment. Jack headed to the stool at the far end of the bar.

"Whiskey. Neat." He slapped down a handful of bills.

The glass barely touched the wood before he downed it in one swallow.

"Again."

He repeated the process two more times before pausing. The bartender hurried to the other end of the bar. Jack swirled his drink and smiled wryly.

I'll sleep tonight.

No one came near him as he sat and drank. Jack kept throwing bills down, but his glass never stayed full for long. He didn't talk. He didn't look up. He just drank.

An hour later, Jack was ready to go. He licked his lips and closed one eye as he tried to figure out how many more bills to leave. In the end, he let a few fall from his hands and stuffed the others in his pocket. It took him two tries to stand up.

Just then, the door at the front of the bar opened, and three men with green shirts and work boots walked in. One of them was Terry Bradford. He spotted Jack, and smiled.

"Hey," Terry called out. "Lookie who's here. You lookin' for me?"

Jack grinned.

The perfect end to this day.

"Yeah." Jack stumbled forward. "I've got something to ask. You said something about Patty."

"Pump-me Patty? Yeah." He laughed and nudged the guy next to him. "I bet a lot of guys can tell you about her. You want details? How she—"

That was all Jack could take. His fist drove straight into Terry's face.

Terry staggered back.

Jack grabbed him and heaved him out the door. Bar stools overturned as men rushed to get out of the way. Someone tackled Jack from behind, and both of them tumbled to the ground outside. Terry had already started to get to his feet.

Jack hit the guy who'd tackled him in the groin. The man coughed and rolled onto his back. The other guy who'd come in with Terry remained in the doorway, watching from a safe distance.

Jack struggled to his feet and wobbled in a half circle. Terry stood there, holding his nose. Jack took two steps forward.

Terry pulled his hand down and snarled, "You piece of—"

The second punch caught Terry on the chin. His mouth closed with a pop, but he remained on his feet. Jack hit him again. His head snapped back, and this time he fell to his knees. Jack swayed and staggered. He grabbed Terry by the collar to gain his balance.

"Patty is my *mother*," Jack snarled, and hit him again. "Steven Ritter's my *father*." He hit him again. "Steven Ritter. Remember him now? Did you kill my father?"

"FREEZE!"

Jack looked up. A young cop stood, shaking, right in front of him. The lights from his cruiser made Jack blink, and the police siren hurt his ears.

"Am I that loud when I show up?" Jack muttered to himself.

Jack was holding Terry up by his collar. He let go, and Terry fell backward. Jack staggered but remained on his feet.

"Hands up. Put your hands up," the cop ordered, but his voice trembled.

Jack held up his arms and slowly stumbled back.

"Move away from… that guy."

Terry groaned.

Jack smiled and lowered his arms.

"Keep your hands up!" The cop's voice went high.

"I need to put my arms down," Jack said. "I'm too drunk to keep 'em up."

More sirens blared as a second cruiser flew into the parking lot and stopped in a cloud of dust. The policeman who got out was the same one who'd pulled Replacement over earlier: Officer Nelson. The wrinkles on his lined face deepened as he marched over.

"You again," Nelson growled.

"Hi." Jack waved.

The old cop grimaced. "Put some cuffs on him, Kenny, while I check on Terry."

"Yes, sir," Kenny replied.

Kenny pulled Jack over to his police cruiser and turned him around. Jack relaxed against the cruiser and put his head down on the roof. The young policeman patted Jack down.

"Do you have any weapons on you?"

"Nope," Jack muttered.

Kenny grabbed Jack's hands and started to put cuffs on him.

"You didn't finish patting me down," Jack pointed out. "You should do that. Not that I'd do anything, but your boss is watching."

"Shut up," Kenny snapped.

"I'm just trying to help," Jack slurred. "Because, if I was a bad guy, I could just swing around, grab your gun and… BANG." Jack's arms went out.

"Close your mouth." Kenny struggled to cuff Jack as Jack gestured drunkenly.

"Sorry, I'm drunk. Have you done this before, Kenny? 'Cause you're doing it all wrong. Let me explain. You… what you do is you push me up against the car a little. Not like smash my face, but you push the guy into the car, and it knocks the wind out of them and shuts them up."

Kenny pushed Jack into the car.

Jack laughed. "When I said lightly, I didn't mean like a daisy."

Kenny gave him a harder shove into the cruiser, knocking the wind out of him.

"Good." Jack coughed. "That was much better."

Lights and sirens blared as yet another cruiser rushed to the scene. This one was a white Crown Victoria with a bubble light attached to the roof. Following right behind it was an ambulance.

"Damn. That's gotta be the chief," Jack said.

A middle-aged cop in a white shirt got out of the car, and Jack tried to keep his eyes focused. As the chief marched over to Nelson, he called to Kenny. "You got everything under control?"

"Yes, sir."

"I have the scene contained, Dennis," Nelson said to the chief.

Dennis pointed at Terry, who was still kneeling on the ground. "Sure looks it."

Nelson brought the chief up to speed on the situation.

The ambulance doors shut with a loud clang, and two EMTs walked over, each carrying a large bag. One headed toward Terry, the other toward Jack.

"Evening, Kenny." The EMT set down his emergency bag. He looked to be early fifties, five foot ten and trim, with salt-and-pepper hair and a handlebar mustache.

"Hey, Dale."

Dale put rubber gloves on as he looked at Jack. "Where are you hurt?"

"I'm just tired." Jack grinned lopsidedly.

"You're obviously drunk. But you're cut as well."

Jack stumbled as he looked himself over for any cuts. "No, I'm not."

Dale pointed at Jack's shirt. "You're bleeding."

"It's not my blood." Jack jerked his head in Terry's direction. "It's his."

"Sir, do you require medical assistance?" Dale asked, now obviously annoyed.

"Yeah." Jack nodded. "Do you have something so I can sleep? Some kinda pill?"

"Who?" the chief yelled at Terry.

Jack looked over.

Terry was gesturing wildly, but Jack couldn't hear what he was saying. Then Terry pointed at Jack, and everyone turned to stare.

"Oh, crap." Jack groaned. "That's not good."

The chief stormed over to Jack, followed closely by Nelson. The chief was about five eight with a large pot belly. Sandy-brown hair poked out from under his blue cap. As he searched Jack's face, his eyes went wide. "I'll be damned," he muttered.

"What?"

The chief grabbed Jack's wallet from Kenny. He flipped it open to reveal the license and badge. "Jack Stratton? You're on the job? Darrington?"

"I *was* on the job. After this gets back to my boss, I'm not so sure."

The chief studied him again. "Is it true? You look just like him. And Patty's your mother?"

Jack made a move that resembled a nod, but because it caused everything to spin, he tried to just hold his head still.

"Wait here." The chief and Nelson walked back to Terry.

Dale grabbed his bag. "I'll note that he's drunk and uninjured," he huffed to Kenny before walking over to join his partner.

"Does that mean I don't get a pill?" Jack called after him.

Dale glared back over his shoulder.

The chief, Nelson, and Terry exchanged words. Terry's face was swollen and bloody. Jack was surprised he was able to stand. After a few moments, the chief and Nelson walked back toward Jack and Kenny while the EMTs looked after Terry.

"But Chief, it's assault," Nelson was saying. "You can't just let him walk."

The chief stopped and faced Nelson. "Terry needs a couple of Band-Aids. He gets worse at hockey. Besides, it's my call, Frank. You heard him. He's not pushing for charges."

"That's irrelevant. We know that an assault occurred—"

"No, we don't, and if Terry doesn't want to say one did, it's over. Did you hear Terry say that he deserved a crack in the mouth?"

"Just because this guy says he's Steven's son doesn't mean we just let him walk."

"No. If he is Steven's son, it *does* mean that. It means exactly that." The chief pulled up his belt, and his stomach jiggled. "You and me both owe Steven at least that much."

The chief started forward again, but Nelson stepped in front of him and lowered his voice. "Stick him in the drunk tank for tonight then. In the morning, we can make sure he leaves town. That's the call I would make."

"You're not the chief anymore, Frank. I am. It's my call." The chief pulled his hat lower and walked around Nelson. "Uncuff him," he ordered Kenny as he walked up.

Kenny looked over to Nelson, and the chief's nostrils flared.

"Uncuff him now, Kenny," the chief said.

"Yes, sir." Kenny uncuffed Jack.

"And make sure Terry gets home okay," Dennis instructed.

"Yes, sir."

As Kenny and Nelson walked away, the chief turned to Jack. "Dennis Wilson. I was a friend of your dad's."

Jack shook the man's hand, but wobbled. "Jack Stratton."

"What the hell are you doing, son?" Dennis put his arm around Jack's shoulder and led him over to the passenger side of the cruiser.

"I'm drunk."

"And stupid. Frank wanted me to take you in. He said that he already pulled you over—"

"That's crap. She stopped. What's his problem?"

"Oh, Frank's got a chip on his shoulder. But don't worry about him—he works for me. Now. Why'd you pick a fight with Terry?"

"Because I'm trying to fall asleep," Jack mumbled as he got in the cruiser.

"Stay with me, Jack. Now, I got Terry not to press charges, but…" Dennis walked over to the driver's side. He pulled the bubble light off the roof and stuck it back on the dashboard.

Jack tapped the light. "That's awesome. I have to get one for my car."

"Good luck. They don't make 'em anymore. That one was my dad's." He grinned. "Just like Starsky and Hutch."

Jack pressed the button. Lights flashed and the siren filled the inside of the car. The chief fumbled with the switch and shut it off.

"Sit your butt back. You've caused enough problems tonight."

"Everything all right?" Nelson called over. He was standing with Kenny and Terry beside one of the other cruisers.

"It's fine, Frank," Dennis yelled back. "Kenny, get Terry home now." Dennis started the car and pulled out of the lot.

"Frank's got an attitude," Jack said, fumbling with his seat belt.

Dennis grunted. "He's a good cop, and he's been on the force longer than you've been alive. Show some respect."

"Sorry," Jack mumbled.

"Where are you staying?"

"Hope Falls Inn."

"That's close."

"Maybe I should go someplace else. She's going to be all mad."

"Who's going to be mad?"

"I tried to find out about her, but now she's pissed."

"Her who?"

"Replacement. She's all…" Jack scrunched up his face and held up his hands like claws. "Roar. Angry. She cried. I hate that…"

"What the hell are you talking about, son?"

"Alice. I ran a background check…" Jack's hands went up and out. "Now she's totally nuts."

"You ran a background check on the girl you're here with? And you don't get why she's ticked off? Maybe you did fall a little far from the tree."

"She didn't want me to come here… but I'm gonna do this."

"Son, why are you in Hope Falls?" Dennis asked.

"I'm looking."

"Looking?"

"For the guy who killed my father."

Dennis sighed. His shoulders drooped, along with his voice. "Is that why you went after Terry?"

"No. He said something about…" Jack shrugged. "I just felt like hitting him."

Dennis frowned. "Everyone wants to hit Terry sometimes. But being a cop, you should know better than that."

"I don't know jack." Jack's head thumped against the window, and he laughed. "Get it? I don't know me."

"You're not going to find yourself at the bottom of a bottle."

"I'm going to find the guy who killed Steven. It's up to me. Cops have nothing. Cops did nothing."

Dennis slammed on the brakes, and Jack caught himself on the dashboard.

"My father worked that case, Mr. Stratton. He worked it like it was his own son who got killed, so don't you *dare* say he didn't do all he could."

Jack leaned back against the window and turned his head to look at Dennis. "Your father? That's right. He was chief then. Sorry. All I know is what I read in the stupid paper."

"Well, you need the facts and not what you read in the papers." Dennis shook his head. "The paper here? Birds don't even want to crap on it."

"Facts? How do I get the facts? You said… Hey! You can get me stuff. Facts." Jack tapped Dennis's chest.

"If you really want to know about it, I'll bring you up to speed. We never closed the case."

"Then let's go." Jack pointed straight ahead but then looked around, confused. "Where's the police station?"

"I'm not going to talk with you about it when you're three sheets to the wind." Dennis restarted the car and drove to the inn. Jack was surprised to see they were already almost there.

When Dennis turned into the parking lot, Jack had to hold on to the dashboard. "Well, I got nothing, so I need help. Nothing. *Nada.* Zilchie."

Dennis put the cruiser in park and frowned at Jack. "Sleep it off. I'll stop by tomorrow."

Jack got out of the cruiser and held tightly to the door to maintain his balance. "Thank you," he slurred.

"Just get some sleep."

* * *

The room door squeaked as Jack staggered through. Replacement rushed up to him, but she quickly made a face as though she smelled a skunk. She stepped back. "Have you been drinking?"

"Drinking? No. I drank. I drink… drunk."

"Jack, I… Can you stand right here?" She tapped her foot on the floor next to the bed. Jack walked in a curvy line to the spot and stopped.

Replacement closed the door, then returned. "Look at me."

Jack pivoted around, his upper body swinging in a wide arc. He grinned lopsidedly as he straightened up to face her; the backs of his legs almost touched the bed.

Replacement slammed both hands into his chest, which knocked him onto the bed. Jack groaned from the impact and landed with his arms outstretched. He struggled to sit up, but before he could, she had grabbed his foot and peeled off his shoe.

"Shut up," she snapped as she yanked off the other shoe.

"I'm an idiot."

"Yes, you are." She walked around to the top of the bed. "Sit up."

Jack struggled to maintain a sitting position while Replacement grabbed him and peeled off his shirt. She made a face as she tossed it in the corner.

Her hands on his belt made him gasp. "Hold—"

She smacked his hand away. "I said, shut up." She yanked his belt open and undid the button on his pants. "Roll over." She groaned as she pulled him onto his stomach.

"Sorry," he mumbled into the soft sheets that warmed his face.

"I have a feeling you will be." She pulled off his jeans.

Jack tried to say something else, but the bed was so soft and he was so tired that sleep finally found him.

20

HOW DID I GET OUT OF MY CLOTHES?

Jack opened one eye and groaned. His head hurt so badly he didn't want to move. He tried to remember the details from the night before.

Stupid background check. The bar. Lots of drinks. Terry Bradford. Damn. Cops. Nelson. I'm so screwed.

He sat up and rubbed his face. His mouth tasted like mothballs.

I need a shower.

He groaned as he rolled off the bed, swaying unsteadily when he stood. His stomach turned. He looked down at his pants on the floor and frowned.

How did I get out of my clothes?

After the chief dropped him off, everything was a complete blank.

He held on to the furniture as he stumbled to the bathroom. He found Replacement in the tub, surrounded by blankets and pillows. She rubbed her eyes.

"You're awake. I hoped you'd sleep longer," she said groggily.

"Did you sleep in the tub?"

"Not too well."

"I'm sorry. I was an ass." Jack held out his hand. "Let me help you."

"Look at your hand."

"Ah…" Jack looked down at his swollen hand, noting the dried blood he was sure didn't belong to him.

"You didn't." She glared at him.

"I didn't start it."

"Who?"

"Terry Bradford. He came into the bar and got in my face."

"How is he?"

"Breathing."

Her eyes widened. "Hospital?"

Jack shook his head. "The cops came."

"*Cops?* Did you get arrested?"

"No."

"You didn't do anything to the cops, did you?"

Jack winced at her raised voice. "No. It was Dennis Wilson, the chief. The guy Terry Martinez told us about."

"Did you ask him anything about the case?"

"I don't know." Jack rubbed his face.

"What? Did he ask *you* anything?"

"I screwed up." He leaned against the sink. "I can't remember. I'm an idiot."

"Yeah. You said that, and I still agree. Go soak your head." She removed the bedding from the tub and carried it out.

Jack took his time in the shower. He stayed there until the last of the hot water ran out. He still didn't want to get out. But eventually the cold water won, and Jack retreated from his sanctuary. As he turned off the water, he heard voices in the room. He quickly put on his pants and opened the bathroom door.

Chief Dennis Wilson sat in the chair, and Replacement was on the edge of the bed.

Dennis stood and stared at Jack. "Damn, boy. You really do look just like your old man." He stuck out his hand. "I was talking to your girl here, and she told me you ain't been sleeping. You've been having nightmares and such, so you decided to go looking for your father."

Jack shook the man's hand. He resisted the urge to look at Replacement. "Sorry about last night."

"You've got nothing to be sorry for. I heard what he said about Patty. Sounds like he deserved a punch in the jaw."

Jack just nodded.

"I was Steve's friend, Jack. If you need help, just ask. He'd have done anything for me. What can I do for you?"

Replacement cleared her throat.

Jack held up a hand. "I've been flying blind. Do you know the case?"

"I'm the chief—of course I know the case. You got something new?"

Jack shook his head. This time he looked at Replacement, who gave a small, understanding nod.

"No. It's like Alice said. I've just been thinking about it. I decided to come and check into it."

Dennis sighed. "Well, I'm glad to help, then. I don't know if you remember last night, but you said you had nothing to go on except what you read in the papers. So I had my secretary copy the case files. They're on the desk right there."

Jack looked at the pile of manila folders. It was eight inches high. "Thank you."

"But before I give them to you, I need you to be straight with me, and I'll be straight with you. You're a cop and Steve's son, so I'm giving you some leeway—but before you do anything, you talk to me, understand? If you go off again, there'll be consequences."

"I get it."

"Do you? I know your boss, Sheriff Collins. That guy is so by the book, I think he has it shoved—" He looked at Replacement and cleared his throat. "Well, from what you've said, this is a lot for anyone to handle all at once. Are you sure you're okay with it?"

"I got it." Jack rubbed the sides of his head.

"Maybe we should just take it easy. Treat this like a real vacation," Replacement said.

Jack leaned against the bathroom doorway. "Vacation? What am I supposed to do on vacation?"

"You fish?" Dennis asked.

"Fish? Well… not since high school."

"Go get a fishing rod and take a break. We've got some of the best fishing around."
Jack saw Replacement's worried face. "Where?"

"You drove over Mill Brook River when you got off the highway," Dennis said. "Head back that way and take a right before the bridge. There's a little pond. Your dad and I used to go there all the time. There's a path that goes all the way around. On the right are two large rocks, and right there is the deep spot. Catfish big as your arm."

"Got it."

"A little before the bridge is Ron's Bait, Tackle, and Sports. You can get some gear there. After you go fishing, if you still want to, we'll talk."

"Okay."

Dennis waved to Replacement. "Nice to meet you."

"Nice to meet you too."

Jack walked Dennis to the door and held out his hand. "Thank you again. I appreciate you smoothing things over with Terry."

Dennis shook his hand, then winked at Replacement. "Keep an eye on him, sweetie."

* * *

"So," Replacement said. "Do you want something to eat before we go fishing?"

Jack didn't think his stomach was ready for food just yet. "I'm good." He moved over to the desk and switched on the lamp.

"Well, I'm not going to miss out on that delicious breakfast just because you're hungover. I'll go down and see if I'm allowed to bring something up to the room. I'll be right back."

When the door closed behind her, Jack just sat and stared at the stack the chief had brought. He wanted to find his father's killer, but he wasn't eager to know what was in those files. Finally, he took a deep breath and pulled over the first file.

He opened it to reveal a crime scene photo. Steven lay on his back. His eyes were closed, bruises covered his face, and his shirt and his pants were soaked in blood. Jack's stomach churned; he snapped the file closed.

God... Please help me.

He closed his eyes and started to shake. He'd looked at a thousand different crime scene photos before. All of them had left their mark, but these weren't of some stranger—they were of his father. Jack wasn't ready for this. He sat there with his head in his hands, trying to pull himself together.

When Replacement returned with a tray of food, he was still sitting in the same position.

"We'll eat something, and then—Jack?" She rushed over and knelt beside his chair. "Oh, Jack..."

Jack straightened up and ran his fingers through his hair. "I've seen three different pictures of my father. Only three." He flipped open the folder. "This is the third."

Replacement quickly closed the folder again. "Jack, I'm so sorry." She touched the back of his head. She picked up the stack of folders and moved it over to the bed, out of reach.

"I need to get through this," Jack said. "I should see the photos."

"You can look at all that tomorrow." She rubbed his shoulders.

"At least let me see the police reports."

Replacement sighed. "Okay. But no photos. And only if you promise to take a break this afternoon and do something else."

Jack nodded. *I can do this.*

For the next couple of hours, they went through the files. Replacement carefully sifted through each folder before passing it to Jack, to make sure there were no photos. Then Jack would read the paperwork, calling out what he felt were important details, and Replacement would jot them down in the purple notebook. Jack's head pounded, but he forced himself to keep going.

But when they'd gone through everything, they still had almost as little information as they'd had before. Jack paced the floor. "They came up with no suspects. No enemies. No motives. Nothing. And nothing similar, before or since."

"I'm sorry, Jack."

"Don't be. This has still been good. It's helped us to rule out a lot." He cracked his neck. "They couldn't figure it out, but we will."

21

CAN THEY GET OUT?

Ron's Bait, Tackle, and Sports was easy to find. Jack and Replacement headed straight for the fishing section.

"Look at this thing," Replacement said. She picked up a big, floppy hat with mosquito netting. "The bugs must have teeth out here."

Jack chuckled. "There won't be any out now." He picked up a fishing kit made to fit in a car trunk. It came with a collapsible rod and all the tackle he'd need. "Do you want your own rod?"

Replacement made a face as if he'd just offered her a flu shot. "No thanks." She pointed to a female mannequin in a pink wet suit. "That's real cute. Where would you use that around here?"

"Big Bear Run," said a short man with a large smile. "It's just ten miles down the interstate. Deepest lake in the state. Welcome to Ron's, by the way. I'm Ron."

"A little too cold for swimming," Jack said. He followed Ron to the back counter. "I'll just take this and a dozen worms."

Replacement's face scrunched up.

Ron reached behind the counter, then pulled out a Styrofoam cup and handed it to Jack. "Do you want a setup for your girlfriend?" he asked. "I got a great starter kit. The rod's purple sparkled."

Replacement quickly shook her head. "Thanks, but I don't fish."

Jack paid for everything, and they headed for the car. He put the tackle box and rod in the back, and when they were both seated, he handed the Styrofoam cup to Replacement. "Do you mind holding them?"

"Them?"

"The worms."

Replacement whacked his shoulder with one hand and held the container far away from herself. "Gross. Take it back! Take it back!"

Jack took the container back. "I just didn't want it to tip over. Can you put it between your feet or something?"

She scooted over against the door. "What? Can they get out? No."

Jack started to set them on the seat next to him.

"Not there!" Replacement waved her hands and shifted as far away as she could. "Put them in the trunk."

"Come on. Don't be so dramatic."

"They're *worms*."

Jack shook his head, but he went and put the worms in the trunk.

Ten minutes later, the Impala made its way down a narrow road through thick pines. After a few twists and turns, they stopped in a gravel parking lot. Across a grassy field dotted with picnic tables, a little pond sat in the distance. A wood chip path snaked its way through the tall grass.

Jack grabbed the fishing rod and worms from the trunk. As he slammed the trunk shut, he heard the crunch of gravel from back down the road—the sound of a car stopping. He looked toward the sound, but couldn't see through the trees. Then tires churned the gravel as the car turned around and sped off.

"Are you feeling better?" Replacement stretched her arms above her head as she got out of the car.

Jack stared up the road and listened as the unseen car drove away.

"Hello?" She waved her hand, trying to break his trance.

"Sorry." Jack shook his head. "The shower, food, and aspirin helped. Thank you for not giving me a guilt trip this morning."

Replacement's head tipped to the side. "I might talk a lot, but I'm not a nagging shrew."

"Any other girl would have smothered me in my sleep last night."

She smirked. "That thought does have some appeal, but you apologized. All's forgiven, east from west."

* * *

The pond had a little wooden dock, but Jack had decided to settle in on a wide, flat rock that stretched out into the water. It hadn't taken long to set up the rod and bait the hook, and now he fished in silence while Replacement squatted down and looked out over the water.

"I need to go there," Jack said.

"Where?"

"Buckmaster. I need to see the crime scene."

Replacement sighed. "I thought today you'd take it easy. Just fish."

Jack held his hand out to the still water. "I know, but... they didn't dive the pond."

"They dredged it."

"It's not the same. And they didn't do it until spring."

"I'll confirm it when I get to a computer, but the police report said that the pond iced over."

"Still, they should have gone diving. Just dredging it isn't the same."

"Wouldn't it be like looking for a needle in a haystack?"

"Not these days—there are good techniques. You need to search in a grid. Slowly. They have metal detectors now that are much better, too."

Replacement peered into the water. "Look how clear the water is."

Jack looked over the edge, too. The water was so clear he could see the sandy bottom.

"How deep is it?"

"Right here is about eight feet." Jack pointed. "Over where I cast is deeper, I think. Hold on." He started to reel in his line.

"What are you doing?"

"I want to get rid of the bobber so I can bottom fish. It's deep, and look how still the water is. The chief was right: this place is perfect for catfish."

Replacement folded her hands in front of herself and smiled.

"Do you want a turn?" Jack held out the rod.

Replacement hesitated, and he noticed the slightest curl of her lip. "No thanks. You fish."

"You're going to be bored just watching me. Do you want to walk around or something?"

"Do you mind?"

Jack smiled. "We're on vacation, right? You can do whatever you want."

"Thanks." She looked around. "I'll follow that trail." She headed for a path that ran straight up a little hill.

Jack cast out the line again and watched it disappear. He kept his finger loose on the line, feeling it as it continued to slide out. Finally, the line stopped.

When he looked back, Replacement was already at the top of the hill. She saw him looking, waved, and then continued on out of sight. Jack brushed back his hair and made a face. His head still pounded.

The rod twitched in his hands. He gave a firm, quick tug to set the hook, and the rod bent over. He smiled as he reeled in. It was sluggish. He stopped reeling. The end of the rod was curving toward the water. He waited. The rod didn't move.

Dang. I must have caught a log.

He began to reel it in again, slowly, and the line suddenly went crazy. The gears on the cheap reel slipped, and the line started going back out.

The tension is wrong! I forgot to set it.

Jack tried to adjust the tension while he struggled with the fish on the end of the line. He moved closer to the edge so he could look down. In the depths, he could see a massive catfish trying to escape back into the darkness. A sudden crack in the rod caused him to lower the tip and reel faster.

"Yes!" he cheered as he finally managed to drag the hulking catfish onto the rock, flopping and twisting. It was enormous; Jack marveled at its size. He was sure it was the largest fish he'd ever caught. After a bit of twisting, Jack freed his prize from the hook, then gently tossed the fish back into the water. With three powerful flicks of its tail, it disappeared back into the blackness.

Jack shivered as he washed his hands in the water—and then he froze, not because of the cold, but because of his reflection. As the ripples faded and the water calmed, he stared at himself. He realized his father must have done the exact same thing in the exact same place.

Steven wasn't anything like what I thought he'd be. He wasn't some guy sleeping with a prostitute. He was just a kid. Seventeen. I had him all wrong…

Jack looked around for Replacement, but she was nowhere to be seen. Leaving the rod behind, he jogged up the path after her.

At the crest of the hill, a beautiful field spread out before him. The grass looked like waves frozen in time. In the middle of the field was a large oak tree. Jack saw its branches move, and then he saw a foot dangle. He laughed. Replacement had climbed up into its branches.

Jack walked over to the base of the tree and looked up. "Having fun?"

"Jack, this is the best climbing tree ever." Her smile was as open to interpretation as the *Mona Lisa*'s.

He grabbed a low, thick branch, and hung for a moment. He felt like a kid again. He pulled himself up and sat on the branch next to her.

"It's a romantic spot," she said. She pointed to the trunk, where the bark had been removed in many places. "You should see some of these. CR loves KD. Billy loves Wendy forever and ever. It's cute."

"Must be a local tradition."

"I found one that may be something."

"May be something?"

"DJ + PC." She pointed to a large heart that had at one time had three arrows in it, but two of the ends were broken off. "PC. Do you think that's Patty Cole?"

Jack shrugged. "It could also be Penelope Cruz. You ready to go?"

"I guess." She swung down from the branch, and Jack dropped down after her. "Did you catch anything?" she asked.

"Yeah." Jack smiled smugly. "A giant catfish. Huge."

"Where is it?"

"I put it back."

"You put it back? Then why did you catch it in the first place?"

"I just like trying to catch them. It's the hunt. Race you!"

Jack jogged for the hill, slowly at first. But when Replacement blazed past him, laughing hard, he quickly changed into a sprint. She was small, but her little legs were a blur. He was surprised by her speed, and he had to push himself to go faster. He made it back to the pond first, but not by much.

"Crud, I almost beat you!" Replacement bent at the waist and gulped in air. "We need to run more. As a cop, you should be super-fast."

"I *am* fast."

"But you should be *super*-fast." She struck a pose like she was frozen mid-sprint. "Like the Flash. Cops are supposed to be able to run super-fast, right?"

Jack grinned. "That's why we have guns and cars."

She laughed. "So, where to now?" She skipped a rock across the pond.

"Actually, I thought of something. I want to go back over the police report."

"Are you sure?"

"Yeah."

"And tonight?"

"Let's get something to eat at the inn. Or we can get delivery. Whatever you want." He knew she loved delivery. "Hey, can you hold the rod and tackle box for a sec?"

Replacement looked perplexed. "Sure, why?"

"Just stop for a second." Jack walked backward toward the car. "Hold up right there." A grin slowly spread across his face as he continued to back up. Then he shouted, "Race you to the car!"

He turned and bolted.

"Cheater!" Replacement cursed, and she sprinted after him.

Jack didn't look behind him as he ran. He hoped the pole and tackle box would be enough to ensure his win, and he was right—though he was surprised to hear Replacement stay pretty close behind. Maybe he really did need to run more.

When the Impala came into view, Jack skidded to a stop.

"You can't let me win now, you—" Then Replacement slammed to a stop, too.

The Impala leaned at an odd angle; all four tires had been slashed. Jack moved protectively in front of Replacement and looked around. The area was deserted.

Replacement wasn't scared, though—she was outraged. "It's a warning! They want to scare us off."

The corner of Jack's mouth ticked up. "So, we're getting closer. Someone's getting nervous. They're getting scared."

"What do we do now?"

"We keep digging."

22

STEAK AND CHEESE, BABY!

The tow truck took over an hour to get to the pond, and it was another hour before the new tires were on and they could leave. By the time they got back to the inn, it was already getting dark. As they headed up the walkway, Replacement turned to look back at the car. "I'm impressed, Jack. I thought you'd be beyond mad about your car, but I have to give it to you, you didn't flip out."

"I guess that was sort of a compliment?" Jack said.

"Yeah. I mean... you love that car. And you've been super short-fused. So what gives?"

Jack smiled. "Someone followed us out to the pond."

"They did?"

"Yeah. When we first arrived, I heard a car somewhere down the road, but I thought it was just someone backing up."

"And why would this make you happy?"

"Because I'm rattling someone's cage."

"In general, or in regard to investigating the murder?"

"I'm hoping the latter."

As they walked through the door of the inn, the aroma of a roast drifted toward them. Replacement moaned. "Do you smell that?"

But Jack wasn't paying attention to the smell. Kristine Jenkins was standing behind the desk. She pressed her lips tightly together when she saw Jack, but the corners briefly twitched up.

"Head up to the room," Jack whispered to Replacement. "Order whatever you want to eat."

"Are you okay?" Replacement asked.

"I'm fine. Go order something to eat."

Replacement held her ground.

Kristine walked over. "Hello, Jack. Can I speak to her for a second?"

Her? Jack's mouth fell open. *Why does she want to talk to Replacement?* "Um..."

Before he could think of a response, Kristine had escorted Replacement back behind the counter. They spoke in low voices, so Jack couldn't hear what they were saying. Jack waited patiently, puzzled. When they returned, Replacement's eyes were wide.

"I think you should go talk to her," she said.

Jack eyed Kristine, but he didn't move. "I'm not sure I want to."

"I... I'd like to explain," Kristine said. "There's something I need to talk with you about. It's important."

If she goes psycho again...

Replacement gave Jack an encouraging look. "Please."

Jack exhaled. "Fine."

Kristine led him into the same room as the night before, but Jack paused in the doorway. A tray with four teacups and assorted cookies sat on the table.

"Please sit down." Kristine motioned to the couch.

Jack stayed where he was. He pointed at the teacups. "Are we expecting company?"

"I didn't know if your friend would be joining us."

"That still leaves a cup."

"It's for a friend of mine."

Jack noticed her hand shook. He stepped into the room and shut the door behind him.

"I... I want to apologize for my behavior the other night." She bowed her head. "I don't normally behave that way, but there was... something about you." Her eyes searched his, but it was the look on her face that made Jack's chest tighten. "When you kissed me, and I looked into your eyes..." Her lip quivered. "I couldn't understand how it could be. Your eyes were the same as someone I once knew." She rubbed her trembling hands together. "Steven Ritter."

Jack felt lightheaded. He sat down.

"When I first saw you, I thought I was losing my mind. But I thought you resembled him, nothing more. I was being foolish."

Jack stayed silent. He didn't know what to say.

"It was so long ago, but I'll never forget his eyes. When I looked into yours... I knew Steven didn't have any kids, but maybe you were a distant relative. I didn't know what to do. I've always been close with Mrs. Ritter, so—"

Jack leapt to his feet. "The other cup. Is she here?"

Kristine held up her hand. "She is. You're Steven Ritter's son."

"Yes, I am."

"Steve and I dated all through high school."

Jack sat back down.

"I was a grade above him. I went to college and... called it off." She wrung her hands. "How?"

Jack shifted uncomfortably. "How what?"

"You. I mean... Who's your mother?"

Jack hesitated. He hadn't been pleased with the reactions he'd gotten around town when mentioning Patty's name, and he didn't want to see that same look on Kristine's face.

"Patricia Cole."

"Patty." Kristine closed her eyes.

"Well? Aren't you going to say something about her? Everyone else in this town has."

Kristine sighed. "Who am I to judge? I know Patty had it rough. It's just that... that's how Steven was. He had a... he had a soft spot for the hard-luck cases." Suddenly her eyes were moist with tears.

Jack started to rise, but she held up a hand.

"Don't. If I really start crying, I won't stop." She rose and marched over to the far door. She straightened her dress and wiped her eyes. "So. Are you ready to meet her?"

Jack nodded nervously.

A brief, sympathetic smile crossed Kristine's face.

She opened the door, and Mrs. Ritter stepped into the room. The old woman trembled as she approached Jack. Her blue eyes were fixed on him.

"I'm sorry I didn't tell you in the store—" Jack began.

She gently touched his arm.

"I'm sorry," Jack tried again, but the old woman clutched him to her and began to weep.

Kristine quietly left the room.

Finally, Mrs. Ritter stopped weeping and took a step back. "What's your name?" she asked.

"Jack Stratton."

"And who... who's your mother?"

"Maybe we should sit down. It's a long story."

Jack decided to tell her everything. As they sat together on the sofa, he told her about being left at the bus station, Aunt Haddie's, and his adopted parents. The summation of his life took over an hour. And throughout, he could see that the old woman fought to hold back tears.

"I don't understand why Patty didn't tell me..." she said when he was done.

"She was pretty messed up. I don't know why she kept me so long."

She put her hand on Jack's. "I'd never have let you go."

Jack held the old woman while she cried some more. "Steven would have been so proud," she said, and let out a large sob.

Just then the door popped open, and Kristine and Replacement tumbled awkwardly into the room. *Listening at the door*, Jack thought. *I should have known.* The two women straightened up and tried not to look guilty.

Jack grimaced. "Well, Alice, since you're here, there's someone I'd like you to meet. This is Mrs. Ritter. My... grandmother."

Replacement cleared her throat and took a step forward. "I'm Alice."

"Nice to meet you, my dear." Mrs. Ritter shook Replacement's outstretched hand.

"It's nice to meet you, too."

Jack stood. "Well, I guess this is our cue to stop here." He turned to Mrs. Ritter. "I'm sure you're feeling overwhelmed."

Mrs. Ritter grabbed his hand. "I am, for now, but please, I'd like to talk some more later. Would you come and visit? I can make you lunch?" The woman struggled for words as she pulled herself up.

"That would be fine." Jack gave her a reassuring smile, and Kristine placed her arm around the old woman's shoulders. "I'll get your number from Kristine."

"Okay."

She hugged him, long and hard. "It was very nice to meet you, Jack."

Jack relaxed into the hug. "I'll see you soon."

Mrs. Ritter stepped back and smiled, and Kristine walked her out the door.

Replacement and Jack watched them go. "Well," Jack said. "Hungry?"

"I'm starving." Replacement spun around.

"You could have grabbed something to eat in the dining room."

"I waited for you. And I ordered in. It's waiting in our room."

"What did you get us?"

"Subs. Steak and cheese, baby!" She raced up the stairs.

* * *

Replacement came out of the bathroom, ready for bed, and started pulling a blanket and pillow off the bed.

"Don't." Jack kicked off his shoes.

"Care to elaborate?"

"You can sleep in the bed," Jack said. He grabbed some sweats and headed for the bathroom.

"And have you toss and turn all night and have another nuclear meltdown? No thanks. I'll take the tub."

She picked up the pile of bedding, but Jack stopped her in the doorway and held his hand up like a cop directing traffic. "Sleep on your side. We'll put a pillow barrier between us."

"Really?" She squeezed the pillow tightly to her chest so her dimples got even bigger.

"Yeah, really."

While Jack was in the bathroom, Replacement divided the bed with a rolled-up blanket down the middle. Jack slipped under the covers onto his side. As he lay on his back and stared up at the ceiling, he relaxed. He settled into the softness and let the warmth of the bed radiate into his body.

I have a grandmother. Weird.

On the other side of the blanket divider, Replacement wriggled around. The whole bed shook until she was comfortable. "Isn't this bed awesome?" she whispered.

Jack's eyelids were so heavy he could barely lift them. "It is. Can I ask you a question?" He opened one eye to find Replacement's face right next to his. He pulled his face back. "I'm glad they have toothbrushes."

"Me too. It's a really good one. I thought, free? It's going to be one of those that fall apart and the bristles get stuck in your teeth. You know what I mean?"

Jack smiled even as he struggled to keep his eyes open.

"Was that your question?"

"No. I have two."

"What's your first question?" She leaned closer.

"Is there, like, a Grandmother's Day?"

"Aww." Replacement set her chin on her hand, and her lower lip stuck out. "You're so sweet. I'm sure there is. I'll look it up. What's the second?"

"How did you end up at Aunt Haddie's?"

Replacement was quiet for a minute, then closed her eyes. "My parents died. That's it. One minute I was in the happiest little family: my mom, dad, and my two little brothers, Andrew and Alex. One minute we were happy, and the next... There was a car accident. I don't remember it. Someone coming the other way fell asleep. They died, too.

"I woke up in the hospital alone. I wasn't even badly hurt. I just wanted to go home. But they... they said I couldn't." She took a deep, shaky breath. "Anyway. My grandparents died before I was born, and I had no aunts or uncles. So I became a ward of the state."

"I'm sorry," Jack said.

She opened her eyes again. "It's okay. My parents were really nice. They owned a flower shop. They did everything together. My dad treated me like a princess. He'd bring home a flower for me every day. We didn't have a lot of money. At least that's what I was told. No savings."

She shrugged. "I didn't have it bad like you," she whispered.

"Me? I didn't have it bad." That wasn't true, but it felt like the thing to say. "Did no one ever try to... you know... to adopt you?"

"Of course they did. I'm a prize." She struck a funny pose, then her voice became serious. "I was nine when they died. I went... to a different place... before Aunt Haddie's."

Jack rolled onto his back and looked at the ceiling. "Where was that?"

There was a long pause, but Jack could hear the change in her breathing. It was strained. "It was a bad place," she said.

Jack didn't need to look at her to know she was fighting back tears.

"I don't like to talk about it. It doesn't matter. Afterward, they sent me to Aunt Haddie's. She tried to get me adopted. A few times they had a couple come out to look at me. By that time, though, you and Chandler were in the army, and, well, Aunt Haddie needed me. And I really loved her. So when potential parents met me, I... sorta acted a little weirder than normal so they wouldn't take me. If you know what I mean."

Jack closed his eyes hard and tried to breathe slowly. *Life is hard. Hard for a lot of people. Alice has a heart of gold in spite of it. Something happened to her at the first house. Something really bad. She didn't let it define her like I do. What am I doing?*

"You're a good person," he said. His voice was low, and his throat was tight.

"Jack?"

"Yeah?"

"Thanks for asking."

23

THE WIDOW'S WALK

Jack sat at the desk in the inn's small room. He had already scanned the police files once more, and now he was taking a look at the yearbooks Replacement had "borrowed." She was still sleeping. Her arm was draped over the rolled-up blanket that had served as their nighttime barrier. She pulled it closer, and her leg rose up as she purred.

Jack cracked his neck and looked over at her. The sound of her sigh seemed almost too low for her little body; it resonated deep within her chest. Jack smiled, but as he turned back to the desk to work, his eyes caught a glimpse of her thigh. He closed his eyes and turned around, but another soft moan made him rethink.

Don't go there, Jack…

He coughed. Loudly.

Replacement's eyes flew open.

"Good morning," Jack said.

"I, uh… I… you're up," she stammered. She pulled the comforter around her as the color rose in her cheeks. "Good morning."

"How'd you sleep?"

"Great! Did you like sleeping with me?" She froze. "I meant, I liked sleeping with you. I meant you… I enjoyed it… How'd *you* sleep?"

Jack grinned, but kept his eyes on his work. "I slept great."

Replacement slipped out of bed and hurried into the bathroom.

Jack grabbed another yearbook. He'd already looked through it once, but he started at the beginning and carefully scanned each page.

What're you missing, Jack?

He had learned long ago to trust that "check" inside him. Call it what you want— intuition, Spidey-sense, or a gut feeling—he trusted it. Every time he even thought about the yearbook, he got that feeling. So now he studied each face in every photo and read every typed word. His hand stopped on page fifteen.

No way…

Jack glared down at the picture of a man in his late twenties, dressed in a dark suit and tie. His light-brown hair was on the longer side, and he had a dashing smile. *TERRANCE WATKINS, GUIDANCE COUNSELOR.*

Replacement came out of the bathroom, already dressed but still drying her hair. "Find anything?"

"A guidance counselor named Terry. Patty was a kid in trouble. She may have gone to him."

Replacement looked at the picture. "A teacher?" Her finger jabbed the yearbook. "He's, like, way older. What a dirtbag."

"Let's not jump to conclusions, but I'll call Cindy."

Replacement stamped her foot. "I can't believe I didn't bring my laptop."

"It's not a big deal."

"Wait a minute. I want to go check something." Replacement headed for the door.

"Hold up." Jack grabbed his keys and hurried after her.

"Do you think Kristine has a computer?" Replacement said as she raced down the staircase.

Jack thumped down the stairs after her and called out, "I don't think the original colonists had the Internet, so that would be—"

He stopped when he saw Kristine at the front desk, frowning up at him. She was talking to an older man with salt-and-pepper hair and a handlebar mustache. He looked familiar.

Jack clicked his tongue. "That was... just a little historical joke."

Replacement smiled at Kristine. "Was Jack's dad a wise guy too?"

Kristine laughed. "Sure was."

The man with the mustache scowled at Jack, then looked back at Kristine. "Can we speak in private?"

Kristine led him into the room behind the counter, but Jack positioned himself so he could see. Jack couldn't hear what they were saying, but the man was obviously agitated. He spoke in a low rumble. Kristine was unfazed, however. Her lips were pressed together in a suppressed smile, but she just nodded her head as if she were humoring a toddler having a tantrum.

Finally the man put his hands on his hips and raised an eyebrow, as if waiting for her response. Kristine smiled and kissed his cheek.

When they came back out, the man saw Jack staring. He scowled and left.

"I've seen him before," Jack said to Kristine.

"I just heard all about it. He gave me an earful about watching out for you. You met him the other night."

"The EMT." Jack groaned.

"His name's Dale, and he's my overprotective big brother. You didn't make the best first impression."

Jack rubbed the back of his neck. "I don't imagine I did."

"So. Did you guys need something?" Kristine asked.

Replacement pressed her hands together. "I was wondering: do you have a computer?"

"There's one back in the office." Kristine looked playfully at Jack. "Next to the telegraph machine."

Replacement laughed.

Kristine led them through the small room behind the desk, into an even smaller office. There was barely enough room for a desk, a chair, and a tiny filing cabinet in the corner. A window looked out on the back yard and the woods beyond. Kristine pointed Replacement to a wooden desk with a computer.

Replacement's lip curled up as she sat down. "I thought Jack was kidding about a Pilgrim owning this thing. This computer is older than me."

Kristine smiled. "That isn't a high bar to overcome."

While Replacement got started on the computer, Jack decided to see if Kristine could be of any help with his newest lead. "Did you know a Terrance Watkins?" he asked.

"The name isn't familiar."

"He was a guidance counselor."

"Oh, yes. Mr. Watkins." Kristine's nostrils flared. "I remember him now. He was a creep."

"What about him upsets you?" Jack reached in vain for the notebook that was typically in his chest pocket. He grabbed a pen and pad off the desk.

"Mr. Watkins started there my senior year. I'll never forget the way he ogled me. He had me sit in this low chair, and then he would sit on the edge of the desk."

"So he could look down your shirt," Replacement snapped as she continued to type, never taking her eyes off the screen.

"Seriously?" Jack asked.

Kristine patted Jack's arm. "A lot of guys are scumbags."

"Jack doesn't get it, since he's one of the good ones," Replacement said.

Kristine smiled.

"Is this him?" Replacement pointed at the monitor. Jack and Kristine stepped over to look.

"Yep, that's him," Kristine answered. "Looks like now he has a bad toupee. Matches his personality."

"It says here he's married. No kids. He's a real estate salesman now. Give me a few minutes and I'll find out some more."

Kristine touched her shoulder. "Take your time. I have no idea what you're doing anyway. Jack, would you like to join me for a cup of tea?"

"Hm, that depends. Do you have chamomile?"

Kristine laughed.

Jack leaned down beside Replacement. "What about you, computer geek girl? Do you want a cup?"

Replacement didn't even look up. "Tea? No thanks."

Kristine and Jack walked into the other room. As Kristine poured two cups of tea, she said, "I was hoping we could talk."

It's never a good thing when a female says that.

Jack moved over to the couch, but before he sat down, Kristine added, "Not here—upstairs. I want to show you something." She handed him a cup, and her nose wrinkled as she smiled.

"Okay…" Jack gestured toward the door. "After you. You've certainly piqued my interest."

On the second floor, Kristine led Jack to a small alcove where a wooden staircase led up.

"I thought there were only two stories," Jack said.

Kristine grinned. "Come on."

The stairs led up through a trap door to the roof, and onto a widow's walk enclosed on all sides by glass. Just on this side of the glass panels were ornate railings of wrought iron, fashioned to look like vines and flowers.

But that wasn't what made Jack's mouth fall open in awe. As he turned in a complete circle and looked around, he was met with a breathtaking view of Hope Falls. He gazed out over the forest, which stretched off into the distance behind the inn. "Wow… This is beautiful."

"It was the reason I bought the inn," Kristine said. "I've had to have a lot of work done, but almost none up here. It's my favorite place on earth."

"I can see why." Jack turned to look in all directions. A long field sloped off to the north, rising hills sparkled in the south and, as he looked west, he could see Buckmaster Pond in the distance. "Thanks for sharing this with me."

"It wasn't the only reason I wanted to get you alone. I wanted to talk to you about Steven." Kristine placed a hand on his elbow.

"I might need coffee if we're going down that road." Jack swirled the tea in the dainty cup.

"I think you need to know." She walked over to face the forest. "I take it from what you've said that Patty didn't talk about him, and… I know it sounds strange, but—I don't want that part of him to not be passed along."

Tears are coming.

Jack took a step forward, but Kristine held out a hand to stop him.

"You'll hear things about Steven from his mother, and that's a part of him. She'll talk about Steven, the son. And Terry Martinez or Dennis can talk about Steven, the friend. But… well, there's no one else to talk about Steven, the man."

She kept her eyes closed. "Forgive me if I go on, but please let me. Steven went to my school, but I didn't really know him. He was a class under me, and I thought anyone younger than me was… less. What a snob I was. I'd been seeing Bryan Ross. He was a real jerk, but at the time I didn't think I could do any better.

"Anyway, one Friday night, I was on a date at a little fast food place downtown. I brought the food back to our table and I dropped Bryan's drink. It spilled all over the table—and Bryan. I was trying to clean up the mess—and doing my best not to cry at the same time—when Steven ran over. He grabbed some napkins and started helping me clean up the floor.

"The drink had gone all over Bryan's pants. He called me a stupid bitch. And then… Steven stood up and punched him in the mouth." Kristine shook her head. "Bryan ran out to his car and took off. I ran after him, but he was gone. I just stood there, crying in the parking lot. And then Steven came up and offered to give me a ride home."

She closed her eyes and smiled. "He ran around the corner and came back with his bike." She laughed. "Jack, you and he have the same smirk. He said, 'I didn't mean I'd *drive* you home, just that I'd give you a ride. Your chariot, my lady,' and he gave a little bow. He jogged beside me all the way to my house. We talked while I rode. I never told him I took the long way because I didn't want it to end. I fell in love with him that day."

She opened her eyes, and the corner of her mouth curled into a smile. "Steven sealed the deal when we got to my street. Bryan had come back looking for me, and he saw us. He was too scared of Steven to stop, but he drove by and teased Steven about not having a car. Steven didn't seem to care. I asked him why. He looked me in the eye and said, 'My dad used to say, "Never be embarrassed if you do your best." My bike is the best I can offer you. Besides, Bryan was too stupid not to treat you like gold. Why would I care what he thinks?'"

The corner of Jack's mouth ticked up. "That kinda sounds like how I'd handle it."

As they stood there looking out over the forest, Kristine went on to tell Jack everything she knew about the man who was Jack's father. The similarities in their personalities floored him. Many times he found himself fighting back his emotions, but much more often, he smiled. She talked about times when they were alone and the private things they said, but it didn't feel wrong. Jack knew it was her way of passing on Steven's memory. A week ago, Jack had had no idea who his birth father was; now he found himself gathering the stories that fell from Kristine's lips and holding them dear.

"And then I went to college…" Kristine lowered her head.

"You broke up with him before you went?"

"No. We were going to have a long distance relationship. Steven was confident. He was trusting. But he was wrong."

The silence grew, but Jack waited patiently.

"I called him," Kristine said, shifting her feet. "I couldn't do it to his face. There wasn't anyone else, but I thought… I thought I was so smart and so special." Tears rolled down her cheeks, and her lip trembled. "My new friends at college said I could do better. So I broke up with him, but I never said why."

"You never told him why?" The words escaped Jack's lips before he could stop them. He could see the impact immediately. Kristine hunched her shoulders and squeezed her arms tightly around herself.

"He came to see me," she said. "He drove twelve hours straight to ask me, and I still didn't tell him. What could I say? That I was selfish? That I was a spoiled brat?" She shook her head. "He came back again two weeks after that. He said he just wanted to know why. I could tell how hurt he was, but I just walked away. I walked away from the nicest man I have ever known… to a group of girls whose names I can't even remember. Back then they were so important to me." She leaned her head against the glass. "They were laughing, and I joined them. That was the last time I ever saw him."

Jack stared at her reflection in the glass.

"I thought I was so special." She looked up at him. "And do you know why? I thought I was so special because that's how *he* treated me. That's what he always told me. It was him—*he* made me special." She started to cry. "You don't know how much I regretted it. If I hadn't done that, he never would have…"

Jack put a hand on her shoulder. "You told me a lot about my father. I feel like he and I are a lot alike."

She nodded, but her face was still wet with tears.

Jack turned her to face him. "Will you do me a favor?" he asked. "Close your eyes."

She looked puzzled, but she did as he asked.

Jack gently took her arms and pulled her tightly against him. She exhaled sharply, but kept her eyes closed. Then Jack lowered his face until he could feel her breath on his mouth. "Thank you for telling me about him," he said. "My grandmother also told me some things about him. She told me about the breakup. And she told me what Steven said to her about it." Jack held Kristine tightly as he felt a tremble race through her. "Now, don't think, okay? Just open your eyes."

Kristine opened her eyes and gasped. Tears once again formed, but Jack pulled her tighter. He stared into her eyes.

"Tell me you're sorry."

Her lip trembled. "I'm so sorry, Steven. Please forgive me."

"All is forgiven," he whispered and smiled. "Close your eyes again."

As she did, she let her arms slip around his waist. Jack cradled her and watched the pattern of the clouds sweep across the floor. He comforted her until he felt her start to straighten. Then he kissed her forehead and quietly slipped away.

24

CHAT

When Jack walked into the room, Replacement didn't even look up.

"You're back already?" she asked.

Already? I've been upstairs for two hours.

"You find out anything about Terry Watkins?" he asked.

"Super-scumbag. He left guidance counseling after five years. Went into real estate. He's been sued four or five times. Married. No kids, which is a great thing because he's on a whole bunch of dating sites."

"You seriously got all that?" Jack walked around to look at the monitor.

Replacement's fingers were a blur as she typed. "I have a ton and would have even more if it wasn't for this prehistoric paperweight."

"Where does he live?"

"Smithfield. It's—"

"Two towns over." Kristine smiled as she walked into the room.

Jack searched her eyes. She mouthed *Thank you* as she leaned against the desk.

The computer beeped, and a window popped up. *HELLO* appeared on the screen.

"Oh, snap." Replacement groaned.

"What?"

"He's online."

"Who?"

"Terry Watkins."

"How do you know that? Is he typing to you?" Jack's voice was clipped.

"He sent me a chat. I didn't think he'd respond so soon."

"*Respond?* Did you contact him?"

"We need to ask him questions, right?"

"Why don't you ever ask me first?"

"You weren't here." Replacement shrugged.

"Jack, it's okay." Kristine walked over to the other side of Replacement.

"Okay? The last time she sent someone an email, I got hit by a car."

Kristine let out a little laugh before she realized that he wasn't kidding.

"Well, we did want to contact him." Kristine looked at the screen, and her mouth flopped open. "Wait. Why is my picture in the chat window?"

"I had to make a profile," Replacement answered.

"And you used *my* picture?"

"It was the only one I had on this computer."

HELLO? PATTY? popped up in the window.

"What do I say to him?" Replacement looked to Jack.

"Patty? Did you say you're Patty Cole?"

"Who else was I going to say I am?"

"You used my picture and pretended to be Patty?" Kristine said in disbelief. "You should have asked me first."

Jack groaned. "Just say hello back," he instructed.

Replacement typed *HI*.

After a moment, the response appeared. *IT'S BEEN A LONG TIME. HOW YOU BEEN?*

"Can I say wonderful?" Replacement asked Jack.

"No. She's in an institution."

"He doesn't know that," Replacement countered.

Kristine leaned forward. "Type okay. Keep him guessing. Guys like mystery."

"Actually, we don't." Jack shook his head.

Replacement typed *OKAY*, and Watkins quickly came back with: *YOU LOOK GREAT. I'M HEADING TO WORK. R U IN THE AREA?*

"What do I say?" Replacement's fingers hovered over the keyboard.

"Say yes," Kristine said.

"No, say no," Jack said. "If you say yes, he may—"

Replacement typed *YES*.

Jack's hands shot up. "What the hell?"

"It was two votes to one," Replacement said.

"This isn't a democracy."

"Actually," Kristine said with a grin, "it's my computer, so it's a matriarchy."

GREAT. I'LL CHAT WITH YOU TONIGHT.

The computer beeped, and the window flashed.

"He's gone."

"What did you do that for?" Jack snapped.

The look on Replacement's face made it clear that she was completely unaware of the can of worms she'd just opened. "Obviously, because I'm trying to help. We want to talk to him, don't we? So we go undercover."

"Do you know how much planning goes into an undercover operation? We should have gone over what to say, when, how…"

"Sorry."

Kristine patted Replacement's back. "Well, now we've found him. Should I leave the computer on?"

Replacement frowned. "Yeah, if you think this ancient artifact can last the day without melting through the floor."

Kristine rolled her eyes. "I'll call you if he reaches out."

25

PATTY'S SPECIAL DAY

Jack had doubled back twice to see whether anyone was following them again. It was almost eleven when the Impala stopped in front of the rundown ranch house. Peeling paint hung like scabs all over it, and of the four windows in the front, only one still had shutters.

"Are you okay with this?" Replacement cast a worried look Jack's way.

"I'm fine. You've heard what people have said about him. I don't have high expectations."

"You shouldn't."

Jack raised an eyebrow. "What are you not telling me?"

"I just… I was talking to Kristine about Patty, and… there was a rumor around town." She looked up at the ceiling and took a deep breath. "Well, it was more than a rumor. Kristine knows this woman who works at the police station. When Patty was twelve… It was sexual abuse. Patty's mother reported it. She said it was Patty's father."

Jack's stomach dropped. "Did anything come from it?"

"There was an investigation, but… no. And when Patty's mother died, Patty was eventually returned to her father."

Jack looked for something to hit or smash. He clenched and unclenched his hands.

"Jack?"

He shoved the door open and marched across the yard, with Replacement hurrying after him. The door was in the same shape as the house: peeling paint fell in strips, and only three of the four little panes had glass. One had just a piece of cardboard stuck in it. Jack rapped on the door, and paint chips fluttered to his feet. Instinctively, he moved Replacement slightly behind him.

No one answered.

More knocking. More paint. The door finally opened a crack.

"What?" An old man glared and blinked through the partly open door. Thick gray hair sat atop a heavily wrinkled face. He shielded his yellow eyes with his hand and stared out suspiciously.

"Mr. Cole? I have a few—"

Jack caught the slamming door and held it in place.

"You're a cop. Get lost," the man snarled. His lips drew back to reveal browned teeth.

"I'm not here officially." Jack fumed. "Ten minutes of questions." He pulled out a fifty-dollar bill. "You get another fifty when we're done."

The old man licked his lips as if he were looking at a steak. He grabbed the bill, then shut the door. A chain rattled, and then the door flew wide open.

Mr. Cole was Jack's height, but slightly stooped over. His old clothes hung around him like a scarecrow. As the musty smell seeped across the threshold, Replacement coughed and made a face. The old man leered at her. "Why hello, sweetie."

"Don't talk to her," Jack said.

"You think you can talk to me like that, you—"

"Part of the payment." Jack growled and stepped forward, backing the old man up.

Mr. Cole turned and shuffled into a living room. It was sunny outside, and the light was on, but it was still dark in the room. Old, thick curtains hung across the windows. A small TV sat in one corner with a worn chair in front of it. A couch covered in clothes and assorted trash was against the far wall.

The old man headed for the chair. "What the hell do you want?" he grumbled as he sat down.

"I'm here to ask some questions about Patricia."

"Patricia?" There was a complete lack of recognition on the old man's face.

Jack seethed. "Your *daughter*."

"Patty?" He spat out the word. "That bitch took off years ago. Haven't seen her. Don't care."

Replacement started to step forward, but Jack grabbed her arm.

"She's a feisty one." The lecherous grin appeared again. "Is Patty dead? Did she leave me something?" He started to stand up.

"Sit your ass back down and look only at me," Jack snapped.

Mr. Cole's face contorted in anger. He started to say something, but shut his mouth when Jack took two steps forward.

"Did Patty ever talk about a Steven?"

"A Steven? How the hell am I supposed to know that? Why would she tell me crap?"

"Did she ever bring anyone"—Jack looked around the decrepit house with disgust—"here?"

"She wasn't allowed to have anyone over. Ever. It would just cause problems."

"You never knew any of her friends? You don't know anything about her?" Jack's words crackled.

"Spoiled little witch like her mother. After her mother died, Patty ran off."

"Gee. Wonder why," Replacement said drily.

"Shut your hole, you—"

Jack lunged forward and grabbed the arms of the chair. His face was inches away from Mr. Cole, who leaned back, terrified. "Do you know anything, old man?"

"No. No." He shook his head.

"You don't get the other fifty," Jack spat. He shoved the chair and started to walk out.

"Wait. I've got some of her stuff. It's in her bedroom. Down the hall, on the left. You can take a look–for the fifty."

Jack peered down the dark hallway. "Stay right there," he growled at the old man, then took Replacement by the hand. "And you, stay near me."

"Are you kidding? I want to climb on your back."

Jack strode down the hall to the door on the left. He stood to the side of the door and pushed it open. The hinges groaned in protest. Inside, a small bedframe with no mattress sat against the far wall. Two sawhorses and old paint cans were stacked against one wall, some old plywood leaned against another, and the floor was littered with trash. But it was still obvious that this had once been a girl's bedroom. Yellowed posters of musicians and actors Jack didn't know still clung to the walls.

Jack moved to the bureau. Faded stickers covered the front, but there were only some old tools inside—nothing that would help them.

The closet was another story. The door had been removed and was leaning at an angle against the back of the closet. Jack picked it up and set it next to the plywood stack. Two cardboard boxes lay inside. They weren't sealed, but their covers were folded to keep them closed.

Jack opened them both. The first contained stuffed animals. The second one, schoolbooks. He closed them back up, and handed the first one to Replacement.

"This one's the lightest," he said. "Take it straight to the car."

"We can't just take it."

"Yes, we can."

Jack grabbed the other box and headed back to the living room.

The old man stood up from his chair. "Don't bring that shi—"

"Shut up," Jack barked.

Jack held the front door open for Replacement, who walked out to the car with her box.

"You can't take anything," Mr. Cole said.

Jack shut the door behind Replacement, then returned to the living room and set his box down. Then he walked right up to the old man, fury in his eyes.

Mr. Cole took a step back. "Fine. Just take it. Take it."

"Do you know what you did to her?" Jack growled. "People said she was a good kid. You started it. What you did to her—"

"That's a lie."

"You're the one who's lying." Jack took another step forward.

The old man sat down. "So?"

Jack stopped.

"So what if I did?" he spat. "The statute of limitations is long gone. No one believed it then, either. It doesn't matter anyway. I'm as good as dead. I got liver cancer. Doctors tell me I got a month or two. They want me in a hospice. Do you think I'm scared of going to jail?"

Jack put his hands on the arms of the chair and leaned down into the man's face. "Oh, you're not going to jail, old man, and I'm not going to kill you… today. I'm going to come back, though. I'm going to come back on Patty's special day. Do you remember what day that is? Do you remember how she loved that day every year? I'll come back on Patty's special day. And when I do, I'm going to take a piece of you for her."

Jack threw the other fifty on the floor. When he turned around, Replacement was standing in the doorway. He grabbed the box and walked out.

"Jack?" Replacement hurried to keep up with him.

He breathed deeply, trying to get the stench out of his mouth and nose. "What?" He popped the trunk and tossed the boxes in.

"What you just did. Back there? What's the special day mean?"

Jack slid behind the wheel. As soon as Replacement got in, he took off down the road. "Do you really think I'm going to come back and cut off a piece of him?"

"Judging by the way you just looked? Yes. That's a definite possibility."

"I won't. But he doesn't know that."

"He could call the cops."

"He won't. He's a scumbag. Scumbags don't call the cops when they get threatened. It'll take a while to take hold anyway."

"What will?"

"What I said. Did you see the way he smiled when he thought his own daughter was dead but might have left him some money? Did you *see* that? I want him to hurt. I want him to remember Patty." Jack pushed harder on the gas pedal. "He didn't even remember her name right away. He didn't know anything about her. He won't remember any special day. But he thinks that's when I'm coming back. He'll lie awake at night, trying to remember. He'll go over every conversation he ever had with Patty. I hope it drives him crazy, trying to figure out when it is. I hope it causes him to remember her. I hope it causes him lots of pain."

26

JUST WONDERING

Jack and Replacement munched on fresh sandwiches they had picked up at a country store they came across along the side of the road. They were waiting outside Jeff Franklin's apartment building.

"Do you think he knows anything?" Replacement asked.

"He wrote all the articles. Sometimes reporters get information they can't print, but it's still good information."

A small blue electric car rounded the bend and parked in front of the building. Jack and Replacement hopped out of their car. The reporter shut his door and watched them as they approached.

He was a small, thin man, almost the same size as Replacement. His head was bald on top and gray on the sides. With his round glasses, white T-shirt, jeans, and open blue blazer, Jack would have thought he was a college professor.

"Can I help you?" the man asked.

"I hope so. My name is Jack Stratton, and I need to ask you a few questions."

Jeff smiled. "I'm the one who usually says that." He shook Jack's outstretched hand. "Your girlfriend?"

Jack shook his head. "This is Alice. I was wondering—"

"Please, come on in. We might as well be comfortable." He led them inside.

Jeff's apartment was a brightly lit, extremely clean, open-plan layout. Light tan carpeting stretched everywhere, and a tiled kitchen was in the back.

"Please." He gestured to the couch. "What do you want to know?"

Jack and Replacement sat. "I'm doing some research about the Steven Ritter case."

"The boy killed at Buckmaster? Are you a writer?"

"I'm interested in the case. It's more of a personal pursuit."

"Oh, you're a crime enthusiast. My sister is too. Her focus is the Long River Killer. She went out to Boulder and everything." Jeff walked into the kitchen, and the sound of clinking glasses could be heard. "I wrote most of the main articles on the Steven Ritter case," he called back. "It was never solved. Shame, really. I'm mostly retired now."

"Did you personally talk to the people involved?"

Jeff returned, carrying a tray with three glasses and a pitcher. "I interviewed everyone. Most twice. It was the biggest story the town ever had. Iced tea?"

"Yes, please," Replacement said. "Did anyone stand out?"

"No." He shrugged. "To be honest, there was extremely little information to go on."

"I read all your articles," Jack said, and Jeff smiled broadly. "And I just have a couple of questions. What's your personal view of the case?"

Jeff took a sip of his iced tea. He nodded his head as if he was thinking about the question, but Jack got the feeling that Jeff had long ago come to a conclusion about the case and was dying to share it. "Well, Steven Ritter was a Boy Scout. Literally." He turned his hands out. "No dirt on him. No enemies. Believe me, I turned over every rock. Zilch. It's a true mystery. No enemies, and no one saw anything."

"There was never a suspect?"

"None. The police never came up with anyone, and I knew Chief Wilson personally. He worked that case like it was his own son who'd been killed. And I'll tell you what: I think he would have solved it, too. But he died about three months after the murder."

"How did he die?"

"Heart attack, at home. Mabel, his wife, thought that case killed him. I'd have to agree. It really changed him."

Jack sat back on the couch and sighed. "Ripples in the pond," he muttered.

"Excuse me?"

"You don't think about the toll on other people." Jack rubbed his hand on his leg. "One event, but far-reaching effects."

Replacement tapped her glass. "Did you ever interview a Terry?"

Jack cringed, but Jeff just squinted at Replacement. "I don't remember. Where did you get the Terry tip?"

"It's not a tip." Jack was wary about divulging any information.

"Is there some reason you two are looking into the case? Did something similar happen in another town? A copycat?"

"No, no." Jack shook his head. "It's just research. Is there anything else you can tell us? Anyone you know who might have some more information?"

"Well, there's Henry Cooper. He's still around."

"He was the first officer on the scene," Jack said.

"You did do your homework. Yep, Henry found Steven. He might not be talkative though."

"Why would that be?"

"The Peterson drowning?" He looked at Jack like this should mean something. "Father and son on a snowmobile?"

Jack and Replacement both shook their heads. "I'm not familiar with that," Jack said.

"Well, it was big news around here. Brian and Jarred Peterson were snowmobiling on Houtt's Pond. Their snowmobile went through the ice. Cooper was the first cop on the scene. He managed to save the boy, but Brian, the father, died. The problem was, Cooper started talking to a TV reporter right after it happened. She smelled the whiskey on his breath. Chief had to fire him."

"Which chief?" Replacement asked.

"Nelson."

"Nelson?" Jack repeated, confused. "He's a lieutenant."

"He is now. The police chief is elected here, every six years. Nelson was chief for sixteen years until he lost to Dennis."

"And Nelson stayed on the force?"

Jeff shrugged. "I found it kind of odd too. You'd think he'd retire. Now he has almost thirty years. He worked the Ritter case too."

Jack sipped his tea. *Interesting. Another lead to follow up on.* He asked Jeff, "Did you find anything that you didn't print?"

"Well," Jeff swirled his glass and looked down, "there was one thing. But it was just a rumor of a rumor. I didn't feel right printing it." He looked out the window. "Everything about that kid was squeaky clean, but I did hear that Steven may have been 'involved' with a shady girl."

"Do you have a name?"

"Patricia Cole. She had a reputation of being the town trollop."

Replacement blurted out, "Patty Cole is Jack's mother," but the warning came a second too late.

The reporter looked as though he'd suddenly messed his pants. His eyes went wide, and his hand trembled as he brushed his remaining gray hair. "My apologies, sir. I had no idea…"

Jack's tone was ice-cold. "Your articles stopped so suddenly. Why?"

Jeff shrugged. "I wasn't getting anywhere. There was no new information. I tried to keep the story going, but it just faded. You can't really write an article if there's nothing to say."

Jack handed him a card. "Well, thank you for your time, sir."

"You still haven't told me why you're looking into this," Jeff said.

"It's—" Jack began.

Replacement cut in. "We're doing some research for a family tree." She smiled.

"I see." Jeff didn't look convinced, but he let the matter drop. "Well, I wish you the best of luck."

* * *

Jack started the Impala. The engine hesitated briefly before it fired up. He turned his head to listen to the engine, then, after a few seconds, he rubbed the dashboard and pulled out.

"Why do you do that?" Replacement asked.

"Do what?"

"Rub the car."

"I didn't rub the car."

"You did. I just saw you."

"I patted it."

"It wasn't a pat. It was a rub."

"I'm not, like, caressing the car, if that's what you're saying."

"I *definitely* never said 'caress.' Is that what *you're* saying?"

Jack scowled. "She's my baby and she sounded off. I got worried."

Replacement's head wobbled back and forth. "I can't believe I'm jealous of a car." Then her face suddenly turned beet-red and she shifted to look out the window.

* * *

Cooper's address, which Replacement had looked up on her phone, was listed as 43B Westmoore. But when they found #43, it was a laundromat.

Jack looked up to the second floor. "Let's check out back for a staircase."

An alley led behind the building, and a worn wooden staircase badly in need of paint led up to two doors. The wood creaked underneath their feet as they walked up, and Replacement held tight to the rickety railing.

The doors had been scrawled on in thick permanent marker: 43A and 43B. Jack motioned for Replacement to stay to the side while he knocked on 43B. The knock was answered by a guy in blue jeans, work boots, and a dirty sweatshirt.

"Henry Cooper?" Jack held out his hand. "I'm Jack Stratton. Can I have a couple minutes of your time?"

Henry's gray hair was cut short, and his face was deeply lined, but Jack guessed he was in his early fifties. One hand held on to the doorframe; the other he wiped on his pant leg before shaking Jack's hand. "Come on in." He held the door open and stepped aside.

Jack hesitated, but with a quick sideways glance at Replacement, he headed in.

Apart from a door that looked like it led to a bathroom, the apartment was all one room. One half—the "kitchen"—was covered in old, stick-on linoleum squares that looked to be excess from the laundromat below. It had a dingy table and three rickety chairs. The other half was covered in worn carpet and furnished with a fold-out couch, a cheap metal chair, and a medium-sized TV.

"You're his son." Henry picked up some papers from the kitchen chairs and put them on the counter. "Damn. You could be him."

Replacement sat down, but Jack remained standing. "How did you know?"

"Small town. I'm a friend of Terry Bradford's."

The muscles in Jack's jaw flexed at the name.

"Terry's a little hard to take, but he's a good guy. He didn't know you were Patty's kid." Henry sat and put his hands on the table. "Are you really looking into it?"

Jack pulled out the third chair and sat down. "I am. That's why I wanted to speak with you. You were the first officer on the scene?"

Henry's left hand trembled constantly. He grabbed it with his right. "Yeah. You're a cop, right?"

Jack hesitated.

"I heard," Henry continued. "Like I said, small town."

"Was he... was he alive when you got there?"

Henry shook his head. "No. The EMTs came right after me, but there was nothing they could do."

"He never regained consciousness?"

Henry rubbed the back of his left knuckle with his right hand. "No. It was bad. The bastard who killed your father stabbed him a lot. They called it a rage killing. A lot of hate. Didn't make sense. No reason for that. Even now, I bet you can't find anyone who hated that kid."

"The paper said Frank Nelson handled most of the investigation—"

"That's why you don't trust those scumbags." Henry pressed his hands down on the table. "Nelson couldn't tie his own shoes. Guy was a moron. Still is a moron. Chief ran the investigation. Nelson took it over after the chief died. You ask me, that's why they never caught the guy."

"You never had a suspect?"

"Nope. Your old man was a good kid. Well liked. No enemies."

"Did you know him?"

Henry crossed his arms and leaned back. "Yeah. Scouts. The chief was scout master and Nelson and I were assistants. I liked your dad. I don't think he liked me much. None of the kids really did." He scoffed. "I was just out of the marines and was a little hard on them. Kids need that. Most of the other kids were little sissies, but your dad was a tough kid. A good kid."

"You never found the murder weapon?"

"Nah. By the time the state police could bring out a dive team, the pond froze. Nelson had us drag the lake come spring. But there were way too many lily pads, and we didn't find anything. Anyway, I figure the killer just took the knife with him. Why wouldn't he? You want a drink?"

"Water." Jack took out a notebook. He'd picked up a small one at a drugstore earlier; he couldn't be seen walking around with that pink and purple monstrosity. "I appreciate the answers. It helps me if I jot stuff down. Do you mind if we start at the beginning?"

Henry took down three glasses. "I got no other plans."

For the next two hours, Jack had Henry walk through everything that happened after he got to the pond. Jack added to his notes on everyone involved in the investigation and what they did.

When Jack finally closed his notebook and stood up, Henry remained sitting. He looked up at Jack with tired eyes. "Can I ask you a question?"

"Ask."

"Did, ah, Patty tell you to talk to me?"

"No. How did you know Patty?"

Henry leaned back in his chair. "I didn't. I was just... thinking. You know, if she was a kid hanging out at the pond I might have busted her or something." He cleared his throat. "I was just curious why you'd come talk to me."

"Because you were the responding officer." Jack tried to maintain a neutral expression, but he felt the muscles in his face harden with suspicion.

Henry nodded. "Yeah. That makes sense. I was just wondering."

Jack held the door for Replacement. As they went down the wobbly staircase, Jack started wondering too.

27

BAD GAS

The Impala's engine sputtered again as Jack turned the key. He grimaced and pumped the gas until it started.

"I'll have to go get some dry gas," Jack said as he pulled away from the curb.

"How can gas be dry?"

"It's just called dry. It's something you mix with your gas if you get water in the tank. She sounds rough."

As Jack took a right, his eyes shifted to the rearview mirror. An old white pickup truck had taken the right too.

"Where are we going now?" Replacement asked.

Jack took another right, drove halfway down the street, and pulled over to the curb. "Put your seat belt on."

"Okay…" Replacement made a face. "What's up?"

The truck pulled onto the street and came to a stop in the middle of the road.

"We've got a tail."

The driver of the pickup threw the truck into reverse and backed up to the main road.

Jack punched it and cut the wheel hard to the left. Smoke billowed from the Impala's tires as it did a one-eighty, and Replacement was pressed against the door—then back into the seat as the car shot forward.

The pickup was already racing around a corner. The Impala flew after it.

"Use your phone," Jack said as they slid into the turn. "Get a picture of the plate."

Replacement fumbled for her phone as Jack tapped the brakes and then powered into the turn.

"We're in downtown," Replacement cautioned.

"I know. I got it."

The truck's brake light flashed at the next intersection. The right taillight was out. Jack jammed the gas to the floor. The Impala jerked forward and stalled.

"What the hell? No, baby. Come on."

He hit the gas again, but the engine sputtered and died.

Jack slammed on the brakes, threw it into park, and tried again to start the engine. The motor turned over, but the car wouldn't start. The pickup was nowhere to be seen.

Jack screamed in rage. A string of obscenities poured out of his mouth as he stared at the now deserted street.

"Tell me you got a plate."

Replacement grimaced. "No. Too far and the plate was too dirty."

Damn.

He turned the key, and again the engine just sputtered.

Jack got out. "I'm going to try to get her going. When I tell you, give her some gas."

For the next twenty minutes, Jack fiddled with the carburetor, but he couldn't get the car running. Finally Replacement stuck her head out the window and said sheepishly, "Do you want me to call the garage?"

They had to wait another twenty minutes for the tow truck. The kid driving it was Replacement's age, and he was only a couple inches taller than she was. He hooked the Impala onto the back of the tow truck, and Jack and Replacement rode in the cab the five miles to the garage.

The small building was a combination gas station, used car lot, and service station. One look at it, and Jack was sure it was exactly the same as it had been thirty years ago.

"What's the mechanic's name?" Jack asked as he hopped out of the cab and helped Replacement down.

"Marty. He's my dad. I'm Matty." Matty flashed a quick smile. "I'll back your car right in, okay?"

"Thanks," Jack muttered as he headed into the garage.

A man in his early forties, who looked like an older version of Matty, walked out to meet him. "You the fella who broke down on West Street?"

Jack nodded. "It just stalled. It was running fine, but this morning it sounded rough."

"When you get gas last?"

"Yesterday. And I got the gas here." Jack pointed toward the pumps.

"Then it's not the gas." Marty laughed. He looked at his watch. "I have an inspection and an oil change in front of you. You want to check back tomorrow morning?"

Replacement stepped forward. "We're on vacation, so the sooner you could get to it, the more we'd appreciate it."

Marty nodded. "I understand. I should be able to get started tonight, but most likely it'll be morning. I can get you set up with a rental though." He nodded to a blue Volkswagen Beetle sitting outside. "It's great on gas, and you can have her for a few days. It's a little small."

Replacement took one look at the tiny car and pressed her hands together. "It's so cute!" She turned hopefully toward Jack.

Jack sighed. "I don't suppose you have another rental available?"

Marty shook his head. "Sorry."

Fifteen minutes later, Jack and Replacement walked back out of the office. "I just have to grab something out of the trunk," Jack said.

Jack retrieved the two boxes that they'd got from Patty's house and put them in the Volkswagen. "Do you want to drive?" he asked Replacement, holding up the keys.

"Yes!" Replacement beamed as she dashed over to the driver's side.

Jack had to put his seat almost all the way back to fit in. "This sucks," Jack muttered.

Replacement was practically dancing in the seat as she adjusted the mirrors, but she sounded sincere when she said, "I'm sorry about your car."

"Me, too. Let's go back to the hotel and look this stuff over."

* * *

They started with the lighter box, the one with stuffed animals on top. It appeared to be a collection of Patty's mementos: under the stuffed animals were a trophy from an elementary school spelling bee, another one from gymnastics, and a framed picture of Patty when she was only five or six, hugging a slender, smiling woman.

My other grandmother.

The woman looked a little like Patty, but she had a rounder face. Her smile was broad. They both looked quite happy. The glass in the frame was gone, but the frame itself was decorated with colorful hearts.

The other box had two high school math books on top of a stack of teen magazines from thirty years ago. At the very bottom was a yearbook.

Replacement lifted out the old yearbook. "It's from middle school." It was small and yellowed with age. The front had water spots, and it smelled of mildew. Replacement's nose crinkled. "How about we look at this... not on the bed?"

She scooted off and went to the desk. Jack looked over her shoulder. They found twelve pictures of Patty and two of Steven. In every picture, she was beaming.

"She looks like a happy kid," Jack said.

She was *a happy kid—before her mother died and her father...*

At the back of the book, pressed between the pages, was a homemade card—a red construction paper valentine, in the shape of a heart, with three arrows going through it from left to right. "Three arrows—that's a lot of love," Replacement said. "PC & DJ. That's sweet. If she kept it, it was special to her."

"DJ?" Jack looked around. "Those are the same initials you found carved on that tree."

Replacement nodded. "I think you're right."

Jack grabbed one of the high school yearbooks. "Maybe we can find out who DJ is. You check that one."

After a few minutes, they both closed their books.

"Zip," Jack said.

"*Nada.* No names that start with *D* and end in *J*."

"But there was definitely someone. Someone not at her school. Unless they were older?" He considered for a moment, then gave up and sighed. "Are you hungry?"

"Are you kidding? I'm starving." Replacement jumped up, went to the closet, and took out the brown dress. "Do you think maybe we could... go out? There's a little Italian place around the corner."

Inside, Jack groaned. The last thing he wanted to do was be at a crowded restaurant. But he could hardly refuse those big green eyes. Besides, he knew why she wanted to go. She wanted an opportunity to wear that dress.

"Sure," he said.

Replacement's face lit up. She danced into the bathroom, clutching the dress to her chest.

28

WHAT ARE YOU SELLING?

The next morning, Jack awoke to the scent of lilac and the warmth of breath against his cheek. He turned his head and opened his eyes. Replacement's face was right next to his.

Sometime during the night, Jack must have broken through the blanket wall running down the middle of the bed—and now Replacement was pressed right up against him. One of her arms was around his waist, and her breath came in little puffs against his face.

Alice… You're easy to talk to. You're real. Genuine.

The fresh spring scent of the bedding mingled with the scent of her hair. She moaned softly, and her chin rose. Their lips were now only a breath apart. All Jack had to do was angle his head…

Oh, man. Don't. Don't.

Jack tried not to breathe as he scooted backward and out of the bed. He almost ran for the bathroom.

Seriously, stupid, don't do it. I'm the only friend she has. If it didn't work out…

Jack washed his face and changed. He wrote a quick note to let her know he was going for a drive, and left it on the pillow. As silently as he could, he gathered up his shoes, wallet, and keys, and slipped out the door.

Go for a ride. Think.

As he headed out of the inn, the chill from the crisp morning air was refreshing. He breathed in deeply. The first rays of dawn lightened the sky, and a mist clung to the trees and ground. Jack jogged for the car. It was the type of morning that made him want to run. The gravel crunched under his feet, but all around him was still.

He paused when he reached the small blue Bug. It was perfect for Replacement, but man, he wanted his Impala back. He hoped the mechanic would have it ready soon.

The little town was asleep as Jack drove through the streets. He tried to remember whether there was a coffee shop near the inn, but couldn't think of any.

Oh well. Might as well get this over with.

Jack knew where he needed to go, even though he didn't really want to go there. Not today. Never. But he had to.

He headed for Buckmaster Pond.

Get your mind back on track, Jack. Think. Facts. Patty asked to meet him. He headed there. Terry put her up to it, so… would he have picked up on that? Was he paranoid like me, or did he just blindly rush out there? What was he thinking? What would I do if I was a seventeen-year-old boy and my girlfriend called me to meet her at night? Hell, I'd get out there as fast as I could, peeling my clothes off on the way.

Jack paid close attention to the route as he went. About a half a mile from the pond, a little auxiliary fire station stood set back from the road, but otherwise there wasn't much to see.

No businesses out here. Huge sections with no buildings at all. And the few scattered homes look new, so there would have been even fewer out here then. Overall the place must have been pretty deserted.

Jack reached the turnoff to the pond and eased down the narrow road. The fog was dense here, nearer the water, and it clung to the base of the pines.

This can't be much more than a mile from Steven's house. It would have been an easy walk for him. Police report said he didn't take his bike.

Jack couldn't see the pond from the parking lot, but there was a little path heading off into the trees. As he stepped out of the car, he dug his hands into his pockets, and his left hand pressed against his gun. Shivering, he jogged down the path. When the large rock he had seen in the crime scene photos came into view, he stopped.

The trees were larger, but he was sure this was the place.

The place where my father died.

Jack exhaled. His breath came out in a puff, and he watched it dissipate.

It must have been Patty who called 911. No. There was no 911 then. And no cell phones, either. The hair on the back of Jack's neck rose. *So where would she have called from?*

Jack looked around. Across the pond, through the trees, he could just make out a little house with its lights on. He climbed onto a rock that extended out over the water. From there, he could clearly see the small home.

That's where she'd have gone.

He pulled out his cell phone. 8:30.

My mom would kill me for even thinking of knocking on someone's door this early, but their lights are on. Someone's up.

Jack ran around the pond, following a faint path through the trees, until he reached the back yard of the little house. It was a small white cottage, and through a big bay window he could see the light on in the kitchen. Staying to the edge of the lawn, he made his way around the front. He followed a stone walkway to the front door, and, after taking a deep breath, he knocked.

He waited. He looked out onto the empty street and back to his feet. He was about to give up when the door opened.

A middle-aged woman in sweatpants and a T-shirt smiled broadly as she looked Jack up and down. "Hello." She leaned against the doorframe.

"Hi. My name is Jack Stratton, and I was wondering if I might ask you a couple of questions."

"I'd love to help you out, but what're you selling?"

Jack shifted his weight. "Nothing. I'm not a salesman. Actually, I had a question, but you're far too young to have lived here twenty-six years ago."

"Honey, I like the way you talk." She grinned from ear to ear and shook her mane of red hair. "I hate to admit it, but yeah, I did live here then. I'd have been, like, nine."

"Who's there?" a woman called from inside.

"It's fine, Mom. There's a young man asking for directions."

"Shut the door or invite him in. It's freezing."

"Your clock is ticking." The redhead winked. "Ask away."

"Do you remember the night when Steven Ritter was killed?"

The woman's face went white, and her smile vanished. She cleared her throat. "I was little. I don't know anything about it beyond that." Her hand moved to the doorknob.

"Did a girl come here that night and use your phone?"

The woman's eyes went wide and her neck lengthened. A second later, she shook her head. "No," she blurted out. "Nothing like that happened that night. I'm sorry, but I need to go."

"Abbey? Abbey, shut the door." An old woman walked into the hallway. When she noticed Jack, she stopped and pulled her robe tightly around herself. A hand went to her curled hair.

"Please, ma'am. I need to know. Steven Ritter was my father."

The old woman stared at him. Jack could see the debate raging inside her—whether to talk to him or not.

He turned his palms out and looked directly at the older woman as he repeated, "Please."

"Let him in, Abbey," she whispered.

Abbey stepped aside.

"Thank you." Jack lowered his head as he entered.

The inside of the house looked as if it would be better suited to Florida, with its tan tile floor and white walls. The old woman shuffled to the kitchen, which had the big bay window Jack had seen from the back yard. It provided a great view of the pond.

"Do you want a coffee?" The old woman sat down. "That one has cream and sugar." She pointed to a cup on the table. "I put it out for Abbey, but she hasn't touched it yet. You don't mind, do you, dear?" she asked her daughter.

"Of course not." Abbey remained in the doorway.

"Thank you." Jack sat down across from the old woman.

"Who are you?" she asked.

"My name is Jack Stratton. Steven Ritter was my father."

The woman reached for her own coffee cup, but her hands trembled, so she quickly put them back in her lap.

"You were home that night?" Jack asked.

The old woman nodded.

"Did a young girl come here and make a phone call?"

Abbey and her mother exchanged a quick glance, then the old woman shook her head. "No."

"Ma'am, I know Patricia Cole called the police from here that night."

The old woman glared at Jack. "I'm sorry about your father, but don't go calling me a liar."

"But you *are* lying. Patty is my mother." Jack let the words hang in the air.

The woman slumped in her chair. "Oh, son. I'm so sorry." She looked closer at Jack and leaned back again. "Oh, dear Lord. Patty and Steven?" Tears welled up in her eyes. "I'm Patty's godmother. Patty's mother was my best friend. I promised her that I'd look after Patty."

"Can you please tell me what happened? Start with the first thing you remember."

The old woman looked at her daughter again, then sighed. "Patty did show up that night," she said quietly. "She was covered in blood and pounding on the door. I just about went out of my mind. She was screaming that someone was stabbed. But she didn't have anything to do with it. I just know it."

"How?"

"How what?"

"How do you know she had nothing to do with it?"

The old woman looked at Jack as if he had four heads. "She's your mother. Don't you know your mother better than that?"

Jack closed his eyes. "No, I don't. Last week, I saw her for the first time in almost twenty years. And now I'm looking for answers. When Patty came to the door, was anyone with her? Did you see or hear a car?"

"No. She was alone. She kept saying he was hurt. She called the fire department for an ambulance. She was hysterical. The EMTs rushed right out to the pond. We watched from the window until they left, but the police stayed a long time. Too long. I knew it was bad because of that."

"Why didn't you go to the police?"

"To report what? That Patty found a stabbed boy? They'd think she had something to do with it. I knew she didn't. Deep down, Patty was a good girl. She just found Steven that way. Besides, Patty's father was a bastard. A meaner man never lived. I don't know what he'd have done to her."

"What happened after?"

"I drove her home. I made her swear never to talk about it. But Patty ran away a couple of months later. I haven't seen her since. Is she okay?"

Jack ignored the question. "Can you please try to remember if she said anything else? Anything at all?"

"She didn't."

"Did she mention any names?"

"No." The woman pulled her robe tight. "She didn't have anything to do with it. I know it. I knew Patty since she was a little girl, but if I thought she had anything to do with it or knew something, I'd have had her talk to the police."

Jack stood. The old woman remained sitting, but she reached out and grabbed his wrist.

"Can you tell her that I hope she's well?"

Jack's head spun. *The old woman thinks she did the right thing. But if Patty had only gone to the police, she might have gotten the help she needed.* He nodded. "Thanks for the coffee," he muttered.

Abbey escorted him back to the front door.

"Thank you for your time," Jack said.

"I'm sorry about your dad. I didn't know him, but I liked Patty. She was always real nice to me."

"Did *you* see anything that night?"

Abbey shook her head. "I saw the emergency lights at the pond that night, but when Patty came later, my mom made me go to bed."

"Well, thanks." Jack reached into his pocket and took out one of his cards. "If you can remember anything else, please give me a call."

"I will. I'm sorry for your loss."

* * *

Jack walked down the faint path toward the pond. The sunlight gleamed on the water, and Jack gazed across to the opposite shore. A hawk rose up out of the trees. It rose high overhead and then swooped low and flew along the bank.

The morning was beautiful, but Jack felt like a shadow passed over his soul. Something felt wrong. Like a child afraid of the woods, he stood with his hands thrust deep in his pockets and stared down the trail.

The warning of the little girl in his dream echoed somewhere in his mind. .

Jack was afraid. But he didn't handle fear the way most people did. He didn't look at fear the same, either.

He gave the fear a second to wash over him. He felt his heart speed up and he swallowed. Then he yanked his hands out of his pockets and marched forward.

To Jack, fear was an action. And for every action, there is an equal and opposite reaction.

After a few steps, Jack broke into a run.

Some people chose to react to fear by running away. Not Jack. Jack always chose to run straight at fear—and make fear, fear him.

29

TWO CHOICES

As Jack jogged back around the pond, the cool air on his face felt wonderful, and the rhythm of his feet on the path urged him on. The pond's surface was absolutely still. No wind blew the branches of the trees.

When he got around to the other side, he climbed up on a rock and looked out over the pond. The water was crystal clear. He could see at least fifteen feet down, but the bottom was still murky.

A streak of air whizzed past his head, followed by a distant, loud crack. From his years in the army, Jack's body reacted instantly. He leapt forward and landed on his belly. Rolling left, he slipped off the rock he was on and scrambled behind it. Another shot whooshed overhead, followed by another distant crack.

Shot came from the parking lot.

Jack's gun was already in his hand. He was lying on his stomach with the rock between him and the shooter. A rifle versus a pistol—he'd knew he'd lose. That left him two choices: run away or flank.

He looked at the slope of the ground and the small gully that could provide cover. He'd be exposed while he crossed the path, but the trees would help obscure him. He sprinted to the left, staying low, and slid to a stop behind a large pine.

Nothing. No shot.

He dashed from the pine to a huge oak. He forced himself to exhale slowly to get his breathing under control. Then he dashed forward to the next tree, pressed his back against the rough bark, and listened.

Nothing. Damn. Now I don't know where they are. Are they rabbiting, or lining up a clear shot?

In the distance, he heard a car engine. He broke into a run. His muscles strained, and his legs burned, but he sprinted as fast as he could for the road. Branches tore at his face and clothes, but he pushed on.

But when he burst out of the woods, the fleeing car was already out of sight. He debated about running for the Bug, but decided against it. The shooter's car was long gone.

Jack screamed at the sky.

30

JUST A FISH

Jack felt a mixture of relief and frustration as he walked back to the parking lot. The echo of the gunshot in his mind made his skin feel cold. He'd been a stationary target, a sitting duck. He was struck once again by the familiar question every soldier asks at one time or another: *Why didn't I die today?*

As he drove back to the main road, all he wanted to do was keep driving. He'd love to be able to take his Impala out, just open her up, and let her run. Instead, the hum of the Bug's little motor made him feel trapped. As he leaned back in the seat, he felt a slight tremble in his leg.

No. Not now.

He gripped the steering wheel with one hand and frantically rolled down his window with the other. The glass seemed to move in slow motion, but Jack needed it open now. He needed to feel the wind.

Please, not now.

He pressed his face against the cold glass with desperation, as if the car were filling with water. He gritted his teeth and closed his eyes.

Jack!

His foot was jammed down on the gas. The Bug was flying down the road, and he was just a passenger in a pilotless ship. He knew his eyes were closed, but he didn't know whether his body refused to obey him or whether his mind refused to give the command to stop.

He screamed and slammed his foot down on the brake. Everything not fastened down in the Bug flew forward. His body jerked into the seat belt and his chin jammed against his chest, and still his eyes remained closed. The force of the deceleration had pushed him against the steering wheel. He sat there, panting into it. His body was rigid.

As grief overtook him, his body finally relaxed. He slumped over the wheel, his hands now on the dash. His foot slipped off the brake, and the pedal came back up with a faint thump.

Jack opened his eyes.

The road was empty. Jack let the car roll forward, and steered it so it was mostly on the side of the road. His hand continued to shake as he shut the engine off.

You stupid idiot.

He pulled the rearview mirror over so he could glare at himself. He expected his own eyes to be filled with condemnation, hate even. But as he stared at his reflection, he didn't see disgust at his weakness—he saw concern.

I'm going to get someone else killed. What's wrong with me? I'm fine when someone shoots at me. I'm not afraid while I chase a guy with a gun. But afterward I freak out?

Jack looked up at the ceiling.

I can deal with it. I can…

He put his head in his hands and rubbed his face.

Please, God… Please, God, help me.

* * *

Jack pulled into the inn's parking lot just as the chief's Crown Vic was rolling in. Both men got out of their cars.

"You sure know how to get people riled up," Dennis said, walking over. "I was having breakfast and nearly choked when I opened my paper." He handed Jack a newspaper.

Jack opened it up to the headline: "Hunting For His Father's Killer." The subheader added: "Policeman son has a new lead in the twenty-seven-year-old murder at Buckmaster Pond."

"Damn." Jack's mouth fell open.

"You can say that again." Dennis tapped the paper with his finger. "Apparently, 'The son of Steven Ritter is set to break this cold case wide open with new information.'"

"Is this paper just local?"

"Yeah, why?"

"You have no idea what my boss is going to do if he sees this."

"I don't know what *your* boss will do, but mine already called. The mayor wants me to let him know what 'new lead' I found. The problem is, I don't have one. You got some new evidence, and you don't share it with me? I've got to read about it in the funny pages?"

"I never told that reporter I found anything new…" Jack trailed off.

"You talked to a reporter? Real smart."

"It was off the record."

"Yeah, reporters always keep their word. What the hell did you tell him?"

"Nothing. I said I was doing family research."

"He's a reporter. A bottom feeder. Right up there with lawyers. Do you know the difference between a catfish and a reporter? One is a scum-sucking bottom feeder, and the other is just a fish." Dennis laughed at his own joke. "Live and learn, boy. Live and learn. Never talk to them."

"I didn't tell him anything," Jack said. Someone had just shot at him, and now everything was blowing up. The fewer people who knew information right now, the better.

"Jack, listen… I need to solve this case too. I know he was your father, but he was my best friend. I don't know if you know what that's like, but there's not a day that goes by that I don't think about your father. And every time I do, I remember that the bastard who killed him is still walking around, drawing breath. Every time I see his mother…" Dennis wiped his eyes. "My dad didn't live long enough to solve this, but I need to. For both of them."

Just then, Replacement bounded out of the inn and down the steps.

Dennis waved at her. "All right. I'm going to go talk to Franklin about this mess. But if you find something, anything at all, you let me know, okay?" He headed back to his car.

Replacement rushed over to Jack. She glanced at the departing police chief. "Let's talk in the car," she whispered.

They got in the Bug. "Where were you this morning?" she asked.

"I wanted to go out to the pond. Then… I went for a run."

"You look like you went for a roll. You're all muddy."

Jack cleared his throat. He knew how protective Replacement was, but he couldn't think of a way to ease into the fact that someone had tried to kill him. "Someone took a shot at me out at the pond."

"They tried to punch you?" She laughed. "What a dope."

When Jack didn't return her smile, Replacement's eyes widened. "You don't mean took a shot at you like… shot a gun?"

Jack gave her a it-coulda-been-worse grin. "They missed."

Replacement grabbed him by the jacket and checked him over. "Are you okay?"

"I'm fine." Jack held her hands. "I told you, they missed. I chased after them, but they got away."

Replacement just stared at him. And the longer she went without saying anything, the more nervous Jack became. She gripped his hands tighter. "Are you trying to tell me that you *chased* a guy who had a gun and tried to kill you with it?"

"I have a gun, too."

"You risked your life."

"That's my job."

"Jack…"

He expected her to yell. To scold him. To tell him he was foolhardy and irresponsible. He braced himself for her arguments and prepared his mental rebuttals. But when her chin started to tremble, he was caught completely off guard.

"I'm fine," he said softly.

He opened his arms to show her, and she shot forward. Her arms wrapped around his waist. She pressed her face against his chest.

Jack held her and rubbed her back. He let his chin rest against her soft hair, and he closed his eyes. He felt his whole body relax. The memory of the gunshot faded. A sense of relief and comfort swept over him. She made him feel good, and it had been so long since he'd felt that way. He let himself relax into her.

A sudden tapping at the passenger window made them both jump. A tall woman dressed in a short miniskirt and a tight, low-cut blouse stood by the car.

"Kristine?" Jack's lip curled.

Replacement rolled down the window, and Kristine's words rushed in. "He wants to meet now. At the Walmart. Before he goes to work. We go with the plan. You follow me."

Kristine turned on her four-inch heels and rushed to her car.

"Go. Go." Replacement put on her seat belt.

"Where? What plan?"

"Follow her." Replacement pointed. "Walmart."

Kristine zoomed out of the parking lot, and Jack followed.

"Why is she dressed like that?" Jack asked.

"She's undercover. Scary thing is," Replacement said, "she looks a lot like your old girlfriend, Gina. Remember her? The crazy one? She's... Hey, stop smiling."

"What?"

"Don't smile when I talk about an old girlfriend."

"What?"

"You should frown or something."

"I wasn't smiling about Gina. I was thinking about when you chased her out of the apartment. But hold on. What are you talking about? Where—"

"Speed up! You're losing her."

Jack jammed the gas pedal to the floor. The little engine whined in protest. "What is going on?"

Replacement's grin quickly vanished. "Well... You weren't here to ask..."

Kristine's car took a hard left. An SUV cut between Jack and her.

"Crud." Jack hit the brakes and threw his hands up.

"Don't lose her!"

The light ahead turned yellow. Kristine darted through the intersection, and the SUV sped up as if it planned to follow. Jack hit the gas.

But at the last second, the SUV driver braked hard and stopped at the light.

"Damn it!" Jack slammed on the brakes. Replacement grabbed the roof handle. Tires skidded behind them, and Jack grimaced as he braced for possible impact. The sedan behind them stopped in time, but the young driver's eyes were huge and his face was white.

"We're losing her!" Replacement shouted.

Kristine's car took a left and disappeared.

"Why doesn't she stop?" Jack said. "Call her. Call this whole thing off until you explain to me just what the hell is going on."

Replacement took out her phone and dialed. "Terry Watkins chatted with us this morning," she explained. "He said he wanted to meet Patty, a.k.a. Kristine, today. I thought—"

"Seriously?" Jack laid on the horn.

The guy in the SUV flipped Jack off.

Jack threw his door open. "Pull forward—NOW!" he ordered, using a voice trained by the United States Army to give commands that would be obeyed.

The SUV pulled forward enough to let the Bug by. Jack zipped through the red light. But the road Kristine had turned down was now empty.

"She's not picking up her phone," Replacement said. Kristine's answering message clicked on, and Replacement spoke. "Kristine, abort the plan. Jack wants to talk first."

"Use your GPS to find the Walmart," Jack said. "Now, what's this *plan*?"

"Kristine agreed to meet Terry after work. We figured we could go over the plan with you when you got back. I thought we had plenty of time. But Terry must have changed the time."

"But what's the plan?"

"Kristine goes undercover as Patty!" Replacement said it as if it was the most obvious thing in the world.

"She doesn't even look like Patty."

"She's close enough. Seriously—same height, blue eyes. Besides, it's been almost thirty years. He'll think she's Patty since I used Kristine's picture for her profile."

"So she meets him. Then what?"

Replacement smacked her forehead. "Crud. *That's* why she's not picking up. Her phone's in the back of her car."

"What are you talking about?"

Replacement was looking at her GPS. "Take the right up here."

Tires screeched as Jack flew into the turn. Replacement's knuckles turned white on the ceiling handle. "Do you two realize she's meeting a killer?" Jack said angrily. "This isn't a game! Call her again."

"She won't pick up. We hid her phone in the back of the car to record his confession. Like an undercover camera." She pressed some buttons. "I'm connecting to it now."

Jack had to restrain himself from ripping the steering wheel off. "You can't *record* them. It's not admissible! Do you have *any* idea how dangerous this is?"

Replacement's green eyes flamed. "Yes. I do. Kristine does, too. She loved Steven. She still feels responsible in a way. She wants to get the guy too. She's the one who came up with the plan. Turn here—there it is!"

Jack turned into the Walmart. Both of them frantically searched the parking spaces out front, but Kristine's car wasn't there. Jack drove around to the back of the building. He slowed at the corner.

"There." Jack pointed. Kristine's car was parked in the back corner of the lot. Next to it was a tan Audi. The Audi was empty, and two people sat in Kristine's car.

Jack pulled up behind a dumpster. His fingers drummed the steering wheel. "I have to stop her. If Terry did have something to do with Steven's murder, this is way too dangerous."

"We're right here if something happens, Jack. You have to at least give her a minute. Wait. I've almost got it."

Replacement held out her phone so Jack could see. The screen flickered, and the inside of Kristine's car appeared. "It's like a one-way chat, but I can record it," Replacement explained as she turned up the volume.

"No. No, you look great, Patty." Terry sat in the passenger seat. "Wow. Really great."

"It's been a long time. I'm surprised you remembered me."

"Of course I remembered you. I just didn't expect you to reach out to me." He ogled her up and down. "Wow. I can't believe it's been almost thirty years. You wrote that you're still dancing? I mean, that's great. You still have the body for it."

Kristine cleared her throat, and Jack felt the bile rise in his own.

"It pays the bills," Kristine said.

"Listen, I'm really glad you're back in town. So... do you need some help again?" Terry leaned closer.

Jack felt his fists clenching.

Terry reached into his pocket and took out an envelope. "It's two hundred dollars. I figure you'll return the same favor for it?" The way he said it, and the look on his face, made it very obvious what the "favor" was.

Kristine leaned away.

"What?" Terry's voice went up. "I'm not paying more—"

He stopped. He looked confused for a minute, then his face turned hard.

"You're not Patty," he said.

Jack threw his door open and sprinted across the parking lot. Replacement was right behind him. They closed the distance in seconds. Jack ripped the car door open and dragged Terry out.

"What the hell is this?" Terry's eyes darted from Kristine to Replacement and settled on Jack. "This is a mistake. I don't know her. I thought she was someone else."

"Shut your mouth, you low-life pervert," Jack growled.

"You're not the police," Terry said, stepping back. "If this is one of those got-you sting shows…"

"It's not," Jack said. "But I *am* going to the police."

Terry's face went white. He looked as if he was about to throw up. "Wait a second. Just wait. You can't—I—Here." He held out the envelope. "Take it."

Jack smacked it away. "I don't want your money. Patty Cole is my *mother.*"

"Wha—? Patty's your—your mother?" Terry was shaking now. "I helped her, man. I was her counselor."

"*Helped* her?" Jack spat the words. "Patty came to you. She was a child. A child who asked for your help. And what did you make her do for it?"

Terry took three strides backward. "You can't prove anything. I'll deny it. The police won't believe you."

"I bet your wife will," Replacement said.

"No." Terry thrust his thumb at his own chest. "My wife will believe *me.*"

"I bet your wife will believe her own lying eyes." Replacement held up her phone. "I've got a video recording of your meeting with 'Patty' here. I hope your wife takes you to the cleaners in the divorce."

Jack glared at Terry. "My mother came to you for help, and you used her." His eyes shot daggers, and his voice was ice-cold. "I should kill you right now."

Terry trembled. His gaze darted from Kristine, to Replacement, and then back to Jack.

Then he turned and ran.

Replacement grabbed Jack's arm. "Let him go. He's not worth it."

"Damn it!" Kristine yelled. She buried her face in her hands. Her shoulders trembled and she began to cry. "I'm sorry. I tried. I didn't get a chance to make him talk about Steven."

"He didn't kill Steven," Jack said. "Patty came to Terry *after* Steven was killed. She wanted to leave town. That's why she took the money."

Kristine pressed the heels of her hands against her face. "Then… this is a dead end?"

Jack nodded.

Kristine hung her head. "So now what do we do?"

Jack watched Terry disappear around the corner of the Walmart. "We dig deeper," he said.

31

WARP SPEED

"Why?" Jack asked. His voice was low and hollow. They were following Kristine's car back to the inn—and driving much more slowly than they had on the way here.

"Why what?" Replacement's hand touched his shoulder.

"Everyone Patty turned to treated her like garbage." Jack gritted his teeth. "She couldn't catch a break. Her scumbag father. People using her. Then she goes to her guidance counselor and… seriously? Do girls…?"

They pulled up behind Kristine at an intersection, and Jack looked over at Replacement. He saw the hurt in her eyes. *If I ever catch the guy who hurt you…*

"Oh!" Replacement took out her phone and started to type.

"What now?"

"Mrs. Ritter. I totally forgot. I don't want her to read the paper."

"You're texting her?"

Replacement laughed. "No. There's no way she has a smartphone. I'm texting Kris."

"Who?"

"Kristine. She told me her friends call her Kris. Did you know she stops by Mrs. Ritter's every week?"

The light turned green, but Jack didn't move. The car behind them honked.

Replacement looked up. "What? Jack? What's wrong?"

Jack didn't answer. He stared straight ahead. "No way," he muttered.

He jammed the gas pedal to the floor. The Bug sprang forward so fast the whole frame shook.

Replacement grabbed the handle on the ceiling. "You're completely freaking me out."

"I have to get back to the inn."

"At warp speed?"

Jack flew past Kristine's car. Replacement looked out the passenger window and shrugged as they zoomed by. They blasted through a stop sign and veered into the wrong lane. Cars had to swerve to get out of the way. The Bug tilted as Jack hit the next turn, and the rear end fishtailed. Jack pumped the brake and jammed the gas.

When they reached the inn parking lot, he slammed on the brakes and skidded into a spot. He bolted out of the car and sprinted for the inn.

"Jack! Jack!" Replacement called after him, but he kept running.

He raced up the front steps and thundered up the stairs. The door to their room was propped open, and when he charged in, a young cleaning woman gasped.

"Sorry," he panted. "All set. Out you go. Thanks."

She scampered out of the room. Jack rushed to the desk and grabbed the yearbook. He scanned page after page.

Replacement burst into the room. "What the hell is going on?"

Jack didn't answer. He just kept flipping through the yearbook.

"What are you looking for?"

"You said that Kristine goes by Kris, right?" He turned the last page in the book, then flipped back to one in the middle. "And that got me thinking about our Terry." Jack slammed the yearbook down and jammed his finger on the page. "That's *her.*"

"Theresa Cook?" The picture Jack was pointing to was of an attractive girl with big, poufy hair. Then Replacement's eyes widened and she looked up at Jack. "Terri with an *i.*"

"Exactly. She's the only Theresa in the book." Jack clenched his fists. "Damn it, I thought Patty was talking about a boyfriend. I never thought…"

"Jack… We still don't know…"

"It's her."

"Slow up. Just because she's the only Theresa doesn't—"

Now it was Kristine's turn to rush into the room. She was completely out of breath, and she flopped down on the loveseat. She'd taken off her heels somewhere along the way. "What happened?" she asked.

"Did you know a Theresa Cook?" Jack asked.

"Yeah, sort of. The Cooks live over near the dump. I went to school with her brothers, Billy and Bobby. Twins."

"Did people ever call her Terri?"

Kristine's hand flew to her mouth.

"I thought so," Jack said. "Was she friends with Patty?"

"I don't know. They were the back-of-the-class types. They smoked and hung out near the dugouts."

"Do they still live there?"

"Yes. It's a big white farmhouse—just take a left before the dump. But you can't go there. Those guys are bad news. Both of the Cooks have been in and out of jail."

"Then you two stay here," Jack said, and ran out of the room.

"Wait! We'll all go!" Replacement called after him.

When Jack reached the lobby, he saw that Kristine had dropped her keys on the front counter. He covertly picked them up and slipped them into his pocket.

I'm sorry, Kristine. I can't have you guys following me. It's too dangerous.

He rushed out to the car. Behind him, he heard Replacement shouting, "Wait! Jack!"

Jack hopped in the Bug and locked the doors before Replacement could get in. She pulled on the handle in vain.

"Jack, don't do this!"

Jack started the Bug and drove off as Replacement turned and ran back to the inn.

32

BEG

The Bug stopped in front of the old farmhouse in a cloud of dust. Jack gripped the wheel and tried to slow his breathing, but he was still almost panting with fury.

He stepped out of the car and headed for the house. Three trucks and four cars were parked around the front, some on the semi-circular driveway, some on the grass. Most of them didn't look as if they were in working condition. Jack's gaze stopped on an old white pickup with a broken taillight.

It was the truck that had followed him around town.

Jack started up the steps to the wide porch. Just as he reached the top step, the front door opened and a man stepped out. He was dressed in blue jeans, boots, and a tan work coat. He looked to be around Jack's age, and he was of medium build, both in height and weight. He was carrying a big cardboard box that covered his face, so he didn't see Jack at first. But when he turned to close the door, he spotted Jack—and froze.

The box slipped from his hands and landed with a loud crash. Bits of glass scattered.

For a few seconds the two men just stood there, staring at each other. Jack waited.

Then the man sucked in a long, deep breath, and his eyes grew large. "Leave!" He sounded more nervous than angry. "Leave now!"

"You're the one who's been following me." Jack stepped forward. His foot crunched a piece of broken glass.

"Are you okay, Randy?" a woman called from inside.

Randy glanced over his shoulder. "Stay inside, Mom." When he looked back at Jack, he hung his head. "I'm sorry."

Jack grabbed him by the jacket, spun him around, and slammed him into the side of the house. "You tried to kill me."

Randy went even whiter. "What? No."

The sound of a car in the driveway made both men look. Kristine's car skidded to a stop, and she and Replacement jumped out.

Guess she had spare keys.

Jack turned back to Randy and glared. He shook him by his jacket. "You shot at me."

"No, No!" Randy held up his hands. "I don't even have a gun."

"Jack!" Replacement called out as she ran up behind him.

Jack shook Randy so hard his teeth clacked. "You know who killed my father." He roared like a demon set free. *"WHERE IS SHE?"*

Randy shook his head. "They didn't kill him. They didn't!"

A woman screamed and ran out the front door. She squeezed herself between Jack and Randy. "Please don't hurt him," she wailed.

Jack recognized her. It was the kind librarian—Mae.

Mae tugged on Jack's arms, but she might as well have been pulling against stone. "They didn't do it. They didn't kill him." She was crying hysterically.

"Jack, please." Replacement placed her hand on Jack's arm.

Jack scowled and let Randy go. "Explain."

"They didn't kill Steven," Mae said.

"You were there?"

Mae nodded. "We all were. Billy, Bobby, Terri, and me. But they didn't kill him."

"What happened?" Replacement's voice was steady.

"It was… We were all—" Mae tried to catch her breath. "My brother Bobby liked Patty, but Patty liked Steven. So Terri tricked Patty to get Steven to go to the pond."

"She set him up." Jack's voice was a barely controlled snarl.

Mae nodded. "Yes. They all waited for him. I liked Steven." She started to cry again. "Patty didn't know. She didn't. Bobby confronted Steven at the fire pit. They got in a fight. Steven started winning…"

Jack's throat tightened. "So Billy jumped in too."

Mae didn't look at Jack. "They beat him up pretty bad, but they didn't kill him. They didn't. Steven was alive when we took off."

"You took off? Why?"

"We saw emergency lights in the parking lot. Someone must have called about the fight. So we ran."

Jack held up his hand. "What kind of lights? Police?"

"Maybe. I couldn't see the car, just the lights. They pulled into the parking lot." Mae wrung her hands.

Jack closed his eyes, and his words were clipped. "Where are your brothers? Let them explain it to me."

"They moved to Reno. I haven't spoken to them in years."

"Terri, then. Let her tell me."

"She can't," Randy answered. "She's dead. Breast cancer. Three years ago."

"I'm sorry," Mae said, tears still running down her cheeks. "I'm so sorry."

Jack glared at Randy. "Why were you following me?"

"It's my fault," Mae answered. "When you came to the library, I just knew who you were. I saw you were looking at the microfiche of the murder. And I told Randy. He's my son."

"I'm sorry," Randy said. "I'll pay for your car. I'll pay for the tires."

"You'll do more than that. You shot at me. You're both going to jail."

"No! I swear! I slashed your tires and put sugar in your tank, but I was just trying to scare you off. I swear I didn't shoot at you. And I'll pay for the damage. But please. My mom had nothing to do with killing your father. And she didn't know I was following you, either. I swear it on my father's grave."

Jack felt as if an anvil had fallen on his chest. He walked down the steps and over to the Bug. He leaned against the car and held on to the roof.

Kristine and Replacement came up behind him. Replacement reached into his pocket and took out the keys. He didn't protest.

"Jack?"

He felt as though she called to him from far away.

Jack looked back at the house. Randy had his arm around Mae's shoulders and was leading her back inside.

Jack hung his head. "They didn't do it."

"If they didn't do it, who did?" Kristine said.

33

GRACIE

Kristine held her teacup with both hands. "Are you certain they didn't kill Steven?"

The three of them were in the little room behind the front desk at the inn. Jack leaned against the doorframe with his arms crossed. "Yeah. A woman who lives across the pond confirmed it. She saw the emergency lights, and a little while later, Patty showed up, asking to call the police. I thought she got the order of events screwed up, but she was right. Steven was alive when the brothers left. They got in a fight, but they ran when they saw the emergency lights."

"The lights…" Replacement said. "Do you think it was Henry Cooper? Frank Nelson?"

"Maybe, but we don't know if it was police lights," Jack said. "It could've been police lights or it could've been an emergency vehicle. There's an auxiliary fire station right near the pond. We need to get a list of who was on duty that night."

Kristine stood up. "I know just the person to ask. The emergency dispatcher back then was a friend of your grandmother's. Her name's Gracie."

* * *

A half hour later, Jack and Replacement stood at the door of a cute colonial. An older man responded to their knock. "Jack? Alice?" He motioned for them to come in. "I'm Thomas Hickoring. You're here to see my Gracie."

"Yes," Jack said. "Thank you, sir."

The house was bright and cheery, with polished wood floors. As they entered, Jack could smell cinnamon and apples cooking, and even though he wasn't hungry, his stomach growled. Thomas walked ahead of them and held open a glass-paned door that led into a carpeted family room. An older woman sat inside on a loveseat, her hands folded in her lap. She had on a plain blue dress, and one leg was propped up on a footstool.

The woman beckoned them with both hands. "Come in," she said. "I'm so sorry I can't get up just yet."

"Not at all, ma'am," Jack replied. "I'm sorry to be bothering you. I didn't know…"

"Sit right down here. You must be Jack, and this must be Alice."

"Yes, ma'am," Replacement said. She took a seat on the loveseat right next to the old woman. Jack settled down on a high-backed chair, and Thomas took a chair next to his wife.

"Can I get you anything?" Thomas asked. "Something to eat?"

"No, thank you, sir. I only have a few questions."

"You take your time, son." Thomas reached out and squeezed his wife's hands. "We go to church with your grandmother. If there's anything we can do, anything at all…"

Gracie patted his leg. "My Thomas has a caring heart. We knew your father, Jack. He was a lovely boy."

"Thank you, ma'am. You were the police dispatcher?"

"Oh, I was the dispatcher for everything," she said. "Police, fire, and the EMTs. Not to mention secretary, log keeper, bottle washer…" She smiled.

"Did you take the emergency call that night?"

She nodded. "It was a young girl. She was just about hysterical. I couldn't make everything out, but I called Henry and the fire station to send the ambulance. The systems weren't connected then, so I had to call them both individually."

"Did you get any calls *before* that one? One about a fight or any sort of disturbance at Buckmaster Pond?"

"No. It was a real quiet day, and an even quieter night."

"I read the report about the call. Henry Cooper was on patrol that night?"

"Yes."

"What kind of man is Henry?"

Jack's question caused Gracie to frown. "Henry is a troubled soul. I hope and pray for him, but he's always battled his own demons: drink, women, anger. He has a lot of flaws. We all do."

"And Frank Nelson came out to Buckmaster too?"

"Of course. Frank takes his job very seriously. He said he sleeps with the police scanner next to his bed."

"Do you know Frank well?"

"He's a fine man." Gracie smiled. "I've known him for almost thirty-five years. We worked together for twenty. He's dedicated his life to community service. I think that's why he never married."

"Does he live alone?"

"He's got a place over on Forester Avenue," Thomas said.

"Did Frank take a cruiser home with him?"

"Yes," said Gracie. "We had three cruisers at that time. They usually left one at the station, but Henry and Frank took theirs home."

Replacement cut in. "Was the third police car at the station that night?"

"No."

Jack and Replacement exchanged a glance. "Where was it?" Jack asked.

"The chief and I had it," Thomas said. "We went to Pinkerton for a conference."

"And you're sure it was that same day?"

"Sure I'm sure." Thomas nodded emphatically. "I was on the auxiliary force then. The chief was giving a talk to the volunteers in Pinkerton and asked me to come with him. We were there when Gracie got a hold of me to tell me about what happened at the pond, and I told the chief. He drove back here like a bat outta hell. I've never been in a car going that fast. That man loved your father."

Gracie squeezed Thomas's hand. "Thomas did too. Steven was in his scout troop."

Thomas snapped his fingers and got up. "I've got something for you, Jack." He hurried out of the room.

"There's a little auxiliary fire station out near Buckmaster," Jack said to Gracie. "Was it manned that night?"

"Oh, no. They just kept a truck out there. Back then, emergency services were all volunteers."

"Would you happen to know if I could get a list of who the volunteers were?"

Gracie sighed. "Well, I suppose I can write one up for you. It may take a couple of hours, and I'd like to call around." She tapped the side of her head. "The old brain power plant's not what it used to be."

Thomas returned, carrying a wooden plaque. He held it out to Jack. "This is from back in Steven's scouting days. Take a look."

Jack took it. Mounted on the left side was a compass, and on the right was an engraved jackknife. In the middle was a picture of a scout troop.

Thomas pointed. "There's Steven right there. And in the back row, there's the chief, Frank Nelson, and Henry Cooper. And on the end there, that's Kristine's brother, Dale."

"He's an EMT," Gracie added.

"I'm not in the photo, because I was taking the picture," Thomas said. "But I loved those boys. Anyway," he looked up at Jack, "I'd like you to have it."

Jack held the board with both hands. "Thank you for this. It's very important to me."

34

JACKED UP

"How's my car?" Jack asked.

Jack had insisted they head for the garage as soon as they left Gracie's. Now they were staring up at the Impala, which was on a lift. Its gas tank was off, which wasn't a good sign.

"It's jacked up," Marty said. "It was sugar in the gas tank. Good news is, whoever did it *really* hates you. They used so much sugar it gunked up the gas lines before too much got to the engine. So you lucked out there—I don't think it damaged the engine. But we still have to flush everything out, and I should replace the lines."

"How long?"

Marty wiped his hands on a greasy rag. "At least a couple days."

Jack didn't want to ask the next question. "How much?"

"It ain't gonna be cheap." Marty looked back at the car. "The engine's got a lot of miles on her. You might want to think about—"

"Nope. Fix her."

Marty smiled. "I understand."

"Officer Stratton?" Marty's son, Matty, was peering at something under the back bumper. "I think you should see this."

Jack didn't like the sound of that. He ducked under the car and looked up. "What is it?"

Matty pointed at a small black box. "Here. Is this some kind of hide-a-key? I went to take it off, but the magnet is really strong." To demonstrate, he started to pull at it.

"Don't." Jack's voice was low and commanding.

Matty's hand froze.

Jack forced a smile. "I'm an officer in Darrington, and we all have GPS on our off-duty cars." He patted Matty on his back as he lied.

"They track you off duty, too? That sucks." Matty rolled his eyes.

Jack turned back to Marty. "Well, thank you for your time. Let me know when it's done."

"Will do."

Jack and Replacement walked across the lot to the little blue Bug.

"Do you want to drive?" Jack held up the keys.

She took the keys and headed for the driver's side.

As Jack walked around the back of the car, he squatted down by the rear as if he was tying his shoe. Then he reached under the bumper and felt around. His fingers found another box.

Someone else has been following me too.

Jack walked around and got in the passenger seat.

"Where to?" Replacement asked.

"Ron's Bait, Tackle, and Sports."

Replacement pulled out and headed north. Traffic was light, and she appeared to relax behind the wheel. But after a few miles, her light drumming on the steering wheel turned into more aggressive strikes.

"Someone put a GPS on your car?" she asked. She didn't look at Jack.

"They put one on this car too."

"What?" Replacement looked down as if she were now sitting on a bomb.

"It's actually a good thing."

"A good thing?" Her voice went high. "I don't see how that can be a good thing."

"I'm going to use it."

"Is that why we're going to Ron's?"

"That's part of it."

"Is the person following us now?"

"I hope so. I want them to know I went to Ron's."

"What're we getting there?"

"I have a list."

* * *

Ron adjusted his glasses as he read down the list of equipment that Jack needed. "I've got everything except the dry suit," he said. "You could try Finneran's Scuba in Yardborough. It's about four hours up north." Ron glanced at his watch. "But they'd be closed by the time you get there."

Jack shook his head. "That won't work. I'm going at first light."

Replacement's mouth dropped open. "You're planning on going scuba diving? Where?"

"Buckmaster."

Her eyes widened. "You're going to look for it."

Jack nodded.

"Why do you need a dry suit? Can't you use a wet suit?"

"No. The water's too cold."

Ron leaned against the counter. "You could use a wet suit and just duct tape the wrists and openings. You can put some really warm water down the suit, and you should be good to go for twenty or twenty-five minutes. I wouldn't push it more than that."

"Twenty-five at a time?"

"Yeah, but make sure you warm up in between. Otherwise you're risking hypothermia, a frozen regulator, or a host of other bad things that you don't want to happen when you're underwater."

"What about the regulator? You have an ice regulator?"

Ron nodded. "I got one. Still, keep the dive to twenty-five minutes. Any more and you're asking for problems."

Jack grabbed a roll of duct tape. "Great. I'll take the wet suit in petite."

Ron and Replacement both looked confused.

"Alice." Jack lowered his voice and put his hand on her shoulder. "I didn't plan on going myself. I need you to go in for me."

Replacement shook as though someone had hit her with a Taser. "Me?" she gasped. "I can't even swim."

"You don't have to swim. You just have to hold on to a rope while I lower you into the water."

"Lower me into the water? Freezing cold water? Are you crazy?"

Jack laughed.

She slammed both hands into his chest. When he laughed harder, she understood. "You big jerk! You were just messing with me!" She punched him in the arm.

Jack laughed again, then handed Ron his credit card. "I'll take one men's wet suit made to fit a big jerk, please."

35

A PIECE OF GARBAGE

Thick gray clouds swirled overhead. Even though the sun had risen, it was still dark and gloomy. Because of the GPS on the Bug, Jack was driving Kristine's car; he didn't want to be followed this morning.

When he reached the gravel parking lot of Buckmaster Pond, he pulled his heavy duffel bag of gear out of the back seat and jogged down the path. He stopped at the spot where his father was murdered. His breath hung in the still morning air.

He closed his eyes and pictured the scene that had happened here twenty-six years earlier. Despite the passage of time, he could see it clearly now.

He had put all the pieces in place.

"I know who did it," Jack whispered. "I just can't prove it." He shifted the bag on his shoulder. "But I will."

***

Jack looked over his diving gear. He had spread everything out on the flat rock at the edge of the pond. He tied one end of the thick fishing line to the seven-inch jackknife. The only thing on the line was a weight, suspended with a round eyelet. He tested the weight to make sure it would slide along the line.

Toss the knife out and use the weight to follow the line to where it lands. It should work.

Jack stood and threw the knife underhand, as though he was throwing away a piece of garbage. The knife splashed into the water, and the fishing line played out behind it. Then he stripped down to his underwear. Shivering, he put on the suit and taped all the seams. He couldn't tell about the hood seam, but it would have to do.

He poured two thermoses of hot water inside the suit, then grabbed his tank and mask. He wasn't that experienced, but he'd gotten his dive certification a while ago, and he was comfortable with the basics. As he sat on the edge of the rock, he checked his regulator, compass, light, and the small metal detector in his left hand.

He looked out over the still water, then bowed his head. "God, please," he whispered, and slid into the water.

The pond was deep, and the sides dropped off sharply. It was like a tall cup that ended in a round base. But it was crystal-clear, and the light filtered through to the silty bottom.

Jack followed the fishing line to the knife he'd thrown. Then he began his search for the other knife. The murder weapon.

It was a rage killing. He stabbed him multiple times. Was his hate satisfied?

The faint ping from the metal detector would occasionally get louder, but from all his years of fishing, Jack had known he'd get lots of false leads. His search grid expanded outward.

Soon he felt the cold water on his back.

Damn.

He checked his watch. Eleven minutes. He was on borrowed time now. He kept moving, working the grid that he had laid out in his head. At the end of a line, he'd turn ninety degrees and move forward.

Sixteen minutes. His chest was now starting to hurt from the cold, and he knew his motor skills would be slowing soon. He pushed on, but he forced himself to move carefully.

Twenty-two minutes. He was past the mark he had set for himself. His hands trembled, and his breathing was getting ragged. He was nearing the edges of the deep section of the pond, but he was rushing now.

You gotta go, Jack. Just one more pass.

Twenty-five minutes. And when he checked his watch, he saw that his whole arm was vibrating.

Damn. I'm done.

BEEP.

He was just pushing off the bottom when he heard the ping. He frantically turned himself around. Dirt and silt blocked his vision where he'd stirred up the bottom.

Idiot!

He swept the metal detector around until the beep was solid once more. He followed it, pinpointed it, reached out.

His hand closed around a long, solid object.

Jack knew he held the weapon used to murder his father.

He pushed off again and headed up to the rocks. His chest was tight, and he had to work to breathe. The water was brutally cold, and now that he was thinking about it, the cold became so intense it felt almost as if he were being burned.

He scrambled onto the rocks and tore at his wet suit. With numb, trembling fingers, he stripped naked and dried himself off. His clothes offered no real warmth, but he got them on quickly, his hands fumbling with the buttons and zippers.

Only then did he inspect his find.

It was indeed a jackknife. It was covered in rust, but even so, he could see that its tip had been broken off. A chill colder than the frigid water ran through him.

He had found it.

36

DAMAGED GOODS

Replacement examined the jackknife. It was in an evidence bag on the desk in their hotel room.

"So… now what?" she asked.

"That's the bait," Jack said. "Now we need to wiggle the hook." He took out his phone.

"Who're you calling?"

"Jeff Franklin."

"The reporter?"

Jack grinned.

Replacement slid up next to Jack so she could listen in.

"This is Jeff."

"Hi, Jeff. This is Jack Stratton. How'd you like a stop-the-presses exclusive?"

"Like a tick likes a dog!"

Appropriate analogy, Replacement mouthed.

"Then do I have the scoop for you. I just have one condition," Jack said. "This story has to be on the front page of tomorrow morning's paper."

* * *

Jack sat alone in his room at the inn. He'd found the weapon that had been used to murder his father. Now he just had to find its owner.

He'd barely slept last night. He was up until after midnight, making phone calls and shoring up plans. Replacement insisted that he get a couple of hours of sleep, and he finally lay down at two.

There were footsteps in the hallway, followed by a soft knock on the door. Jack stood up, rolled his shoulders, and cracked his neck.

Another knock, louder this time.

Jack strolled over and opened the door.

Lieutenant Frank Nelson stepped into the room, followed by a uniformed state police trooper.

"You're wrong about this, Stratton," Nelson grumbled.

"No, I'm not." Jack held up the evidence bag. "Do you recognize this, Frank?"

Nelson stared at the knife. The muscles on the side of his head flexed as he chewed the inside of his mouth. "It's a scout knife. I lost mine years ago. Camping," Nelson quickly added.

"It's not yours." Jack opened the side door that connected his room to the adjoining one. "Everyone's waiting in the other room," he said.

The occupants of the adjoining room—the giggling young couple Jack had noticed earlier—had checked out the day before, and Kristine had happily agreed to let Jack use the room for today's operation. Right now, Kristine, Replacement, Jimmy Tanaka, two more state troopers, and Officer Kenny waited in there. The trooper and Nelson now joined them.

Before Jack closed the door again, Replacement gave him a thumbs-up. Jack winked back.

Everything was now in place. Jack sat down at the desk, once again alone, and waited.

The minutes ticked slowly by. The sky outside was just starting to lighten when there was another soft knock on the door.

Jack got up and answered the door.

Chief Dennis walked into the room. "Morning, Jack." He wasn't smiling. "So, you found the knife?"

Jack pointed to the evidence bag on the desk. Dennis marched over and glared at it.

"It was in the pond," Jack said. "The tip is busted off. I'm sure it will match."

"Nice work. The newspaper said you were sending it to the state lab for some type of new testing. Did you get anything else?"

"I uncovered some interesting witness testimony. Turns out, multiple witnesses saw emergency lights out at the pond the night my father was killed."

Dennis scoffed. "That ain't new, son. Police, ambulance—hell, even the fire department came out there that night."

"Yeah. But they didn't come out twice. Witnesses saw the police show up and leave... and then a half hour later, they saw them again."

Dennis looked down at his feet. "You got a name for this witness?"

Jack ignored the question. "There was nothing in the police report about a cruiser being anywhere near Buckmaster."

Dennis looked up at Jack, and his mouth slowly opened. "Do you think... Henry Cooper? He was the officer on duty. He knew Steven. Cooper's a drunk. He was Steven's scout leader. That's a scout knife, right? The leaders all got knives."

"Shut up, Dennis." Jack's voice was a low growl. "You need some acting lessons before you try that BS story."

Dennis's hands curled into fists. "Watch your mouth, boy."

"Save it. All the scouts had a jackknife. Including you. There were three police cruisers in town. Cooper was fifteen minutes away from the pond. He checked in regularly. Nelson was home. Your father was at a convention."

"You flunked math, I take it?" Dennis scoffed. "You just accounted for all the police cars. So tell me this, Sherlock. How'd these witnesses see police lights if none of the cruisers were there?"

"Because you drove Steven there."

"What? Your old man lived just down the street. He walked to the pond all the time. Why would I drive him?"

"Because Steven suspected something was up," Jack said. "Terri invited him out to the pond, and Steven asked his best friend to come along with him and watch his back. It's what I would have done. And since your father was out of town, you drove his personal car. The one with the bubble light that you're so proud of."

Dennis's face morphed into a deep scowl. "So, you think you have it all figured out?" he spat.

"Most of it."

Dennis's eyes darted to Jack's holster on the table, then his hand went to rest on his gun. "Why don't you tell me all you have then, smart guy? What's this new test?"

Jack shifted his weight.

Dennis drew his gun. "Don't even think of moving, kid. You're not that fast. Put your hands up. Get on your knees."

Jack lowered himself to the floor and held his hands out and up. "I just need to know something first," he said.

"I thought you figured it all out," Dennis sneered.

"Like I said, most of it."

"Ask away. It'll be our secret. Then *I've* got a couple of questions for *you*."

"Here's what I know," Jack said. "Steven went to talk to Terri while you waited in the parking lot. When Terri's brothers jumped him, you heard the fight. You grabbed your father's bubble light, turned the siren on, and scared them off. I figured that part out, but—"

"But you don't know why," Dennis sneered.

"Oh, I figured out the why, too." Jack let a cocky grin spread across his face. "That was easy once I was sure it was you."

"Really, smart guy? Why do you think I did it?"

"Well you see, here's where things get tricky. I know I'm right about this, but if I tell you why you did it, you're going to get so mad that you might just kill me right away. So," Jack flashed a big smile, "I'm gonna need you to promise to wait until I'm completely finished."

"You arrogant little snot. Just say what you gotta say."

Jack settled back on his legs and cracked his neck. "You loved Patty."

Dennis's eyes widened, and then he scoffed. "What? You're way off, kid. I've been with the same gal since junior high."

"Yeah, I know all about your wife. Mayor's kid marrying the police chief's kid? That's right out of a storybook, except it was Patty you really loved. I found the valentine that you gave her. It didn't click at first, because you wrote "DJ." I thought the *J* stood for someone's last name. But that's what they called you when you were little, isn't it? DJ is short for Dennis *Junior*."

"Valentine? What valentine?"

"The one you gave Patty. It had three arrows in it. That's a lot of love."

The corner of Dennis's mouth turned up. "Yeah, maybe I gave Patty a valentine one time. So what?"

"Patty's scumbag father molested her. A police report was filed. And that means that your father looked into it. Is that why you dumped her?"

"My mother told me what Patty's father did to her," Dennis snapped. "I *had* to break up with her. My mother made me. Patty was damaged goods." There was a look of disgust on his face.

Jack fought back a snarl. "So, now I'll tell you what happened. You drove Steven to Buckmaster Pond that night. You waited in the car. You heard the fight. You turned the bubble light on, and everyone ran away. And then you walked up. Steven was lying there, beaten."

Jack paused. "And that's when he told you. Steven told you that Patty, the girl you loved, was pregnant—with his kid. Your best friend knocked up the girl you loved. And the hate just went right through you. Patty was going to have Steven's child. She loved Steven, not you. *Everyone* loved Steven more than you. Even your father—"

"Screw you!" Spit flew from Dennis's mouth. "You don't know crap. Everyone talks about my old man like he was some great guy, but they shouldn't. He wasn't. *I* was his son. *Me.* But it was always Steven. Steven did this. Steven did that. Never me. I always had to bring Steven along whenever we did anything, and then..."

"Then what?"

Dennis's voice was cold. "Steven shouldn't have gone near Patty."

"You have to be kidding, right? Did Steven even know you loved Patty? Did you ever tell him?"

"How could I? My mother..."

"So Steven didn't even know! He never saw it coming, did he?"

Dennis said nothing.

"You're such a pansy."

Dennis raised the gun. "I've had enough of this. Now, you tell me everything you know, and I promise I'll make it fast."

"I haven't asked all my questions yet. You killed Steven—"

"Who are the new witnesses?"

"That comes at the end, Dennis," Jack said. "I'm not done yet. There's more." He smirked. "Because your father was looking into the murder. And he figured it out, too. He figured it out and—"

Dennis took a step forward. "He just wouldn't let it go! He kept on digging. Then one day he came home and... and I just knew. I knew he'd figured it out. He knew it was me."

Jack spoke softly. "How did you kill him?"

Dennis grinned as if he were sharing a fishing tip. "My old man had a bad heart. Everyone was telling him to take a vacation, but no, he wouldn't stop. He had to know who killed his precious little Steven. He used to call Steven his 'other son.' Other son? *I'm* his son. His *only* son! But night and day, that's all he talked about. Steven. I had always known he liked Steven more than me, but now everyone in town knew it too. He mourned him like someone had killed his real son. So I wanted him dead too. I switched his heart medicine. The old fool didn't even notice, but it didn't kill him."

"So you didn't have the guts—"

"Shut up, boy. Like I said, one night he came home and I knew he'd figured it out. He looked broken. He came upstairs so we could talk. He started crying. But I knew he wasn't crying for me. He was going to take me in. *Me!* Arrest his *real* son. So, at the top of the stairs... I gave him a little push."

Keep talking, you fat idiot.

"I hoped he'd break his neck. The heart attack was a bonus. He just lay there, begging. And I stood over him, watching, until he finally shut up and his eyes went gray. Then I knew I was free."

"Until I showed up." Jack clicked his tongue. "It was you who took the shot at me at the pond."

"And you were too damn stupid to leave. I wouldn't have to kill you now if you'd had the sense to just go. Why didn't you? You know I didn't want it this way. You're Patty's son. I tried to scare you off."

"You really want to know why I didn't go?" Jack asked. "You butchered my father. You think I would just go away and let you get away with it? I stayed to avenge him."

Dennis laughed. "You're not avenging anything, boy. They'll look for your killer, but they'll never find him. I'll make it look good. Just like I did all these years. I'll pull out all the stops. I'll call in everyone. Hell, I'll even set my son up to console that pretty little pet who follows you around. I'll make sure he takes *good* care of her."

Jack's cold stare made Dennis shut up. "Here's the last part, Dennis. This is what you've been waiting for."

Jack savored the moment. He let the silence build.

"You're under arrest."

Both doors to the hotel room burst open.

"FREEZE!" Four voices bellowed the command as the state troopers leveled their guns at Dennis.

Dennis looked around, bewildered. Then a look of resignation crossed his face. His shoulders slumped, and he threw his gun onto the bed.

He looked at Jack. "Why didn't you just leave?"

Jack scoffed. "How the hell can I explain it to you? My whole life I wanted to know who my father was, and you killed yours. You wouldn't get it."

The state police captain nodded to Nelson, who motioned to Kenny.

"Cuff him, Kenny."

Tank grinned broadly. "You're still crazy, Stratton."

"Thanks for the assist. Did you hear everything?"

Tank nodded. "Every word."

"Good work, everyone," the captain said. "Martinez and I will take him to Rosemont. Billings and Tank will stay to pack up."

Kristine slipped into the room and held up a slender hand. "Before you go, can you please help me move this armoire back where it belongs? And be careful. It's delicate." She gave the captain a smile fraught with worry.

Kenny had stepped up behind his former boss. He took out his handcuffs. "Hands behind your back, Chief," he said.

Jack could almost hear his police academy instructor's voice yelling at Kenny for poor procedure. *Your feet are too close together. You need to grab the suspect's other wrist to control him.*

Jack started to say something, but it was too late. Dennis yanked Kenny's arm and pivoted around him. He ripped Kenny's gun from its holster. Kenny stumbled forward. Dennis grabbed Kristine and pulled her in front of him.

Jack's gun snapped up, but there was no clear shot.

Kristine froze as Dennis pressed the muzzle of the gun against her head.

No one moved.

"Throw your guns on the bed now." Spit flew from Dennis's mouth. He shielded his body with Kristine's.

"Not going to happen." Jack aimed down the sight.

"Now!" Dennis shrieked. "I'll blow her head off! I'll do it! I will!"

Damn. He's lost it.

The captain held out a hand. "Dennis, calm—"

"Toss them—*NOW*," Dennis ordered.

The captain tossed his gun on the bed, and the rest of the officers, including Jack, followed suit.

Dennis's hand shook. "I need time. A head start. I deserve a head start. I'll let her go when I get out of town."

Kristine was terrified. Tears ran down her face.

"All of you get against the wall. Hands behind your heads." Dennis leveled the gun at Jack. "But not you. Hands up."

Jack raised his hands higher.

The gun in Dennis's hand shook as he pointed it at Jack's face. "It's all your fault. *Everything* is. If you had just left the dead buried… *Damn you!*"

Kristine's expression changed. Jack could see the resolve in her eyes. Her chin still trembled, but her lips pressed together into a determined line. "Damn you, Dennis," she said. Her voice cracked. "Steven was your best friend."

"It was his fault!" Dennis yelled.

"No… it was mine," Kristine whispered.

"What?" Jack said. "Kristine, no it wasn't."

Kristine closed her eyes. "I won't let you hurt his son."

Jack could see her body tighten up as she prepared to move. Dennis must have felt it, too, because he pressed the gun back against her head.

He sees it coming…

Kristine's eyes snapped open. She stopped crying. "I'm so sorry, Jack." Her voice was strangely calm.

"Dennis, look at your chest." Jack's order was crisp and direct.

Dennis glanced down. A red laser dot was centered on the middle of his white shirt.

"On the other end of that dot is a fifty-caliber sniper rifle with the best marksman I know dying to pull the trigger. I lower my hands, you die. I close my fist, you die."

Dennis's face went as white as his shirt, and he squinted as he tried to look through the darkened doorway at the sniper in the next room.

The laser dot shifted to his face. Blinded, he winced and turned his head away. Dennis glared at Jack, but the gun trembled in his hands. He aimed the gun at Jack's head. "We've got a standoff then. I'll blow your head off. We'll both die."

"You won't shoot."

"Why?"

"You ever see what a fifty-caliber round does to someone?" Dennis went even whiter. "That, and the fact that you're a coward, means you won't shoot me. Throw your gun down."

Dennis gripped the gun tighter. "Coward? You want to die, boy? Do you?"

Jack stepped forward. "You know what? I do. Ever since I can remember, I've wanted to die, so I could get out of the hell I found myself in. And that feeling hasn't stopped. It's only gotten worse. Every day, I have to come up with reasons not to eat a bullet. It's wrong that I don't value my life more, but you value yours way too much. You could shoot me, and I might die. But you suck as a shot, so I may not. Even at this range. But that doesn't matter—because live or die, I don't care! You? They won't miss. You'll die, and you don't want to. Now—throw the gun down now or I close my hand."

"You rotten bastard."

"You *made* me a bastard!" Jack screamed. "I had a chance…" His hand shook. "Five. Four."

Dennis's face contorted in rage. "I'm just sorry I didn't kill Steven before he slept with Patty." His eyes shifted to the doorway and the unseen sniper.

Jack stopped breathing. He knew there was no sniper in the other room. It was Alice with his dad's laser pointer.

Dennis pivoted. He aimed for the red dot in the doorway.

Jack pushed forward off the balls of his feet.

The gun discharged. In the small room, the blast sounded like a cannon.

The laser dot blinked out.

Jack's left hand caught the chief's right wrist and shoved it upward. The gun fired again. Jack twisted Dennis's wrist, and Dennis screamed in pain.

Every police officer in the room tackled Dennis to the floor. The gun was ripped from his hand.

"ALICE!" Jack charged into the other room.

Replacement lay sprawled on her stomach on the floor. She wasn't moving.

Jack turned her on her side. His army training took over. His hands searched for a wound while he covered her with his own body. "Status?" Jack yelled.

Replacement blinked rapidly and stared at him.

"Status?" Jack bellowed again as his hands continued to sweep over her body.

"What does that mean?" Replacement barked back. "Am I okay? Yeah."

Jack pulled her close and held her.

Replacement started to shake.

"It's okay," Jack whispered.

"Okay?" Replacement struggled to pull free. "It's *totally* okay!" She jumped up. "You were awesome!" Her face lit up with a grin from ear to ear. "I was so scared when he grabbed Kristine and then pointed the gun at you." She held up the laser pointer. "I was going to try running out to the hallway and stabbing him with the pen part when he came out, but then I had the whole laser sight idea."

Jack's head ticked to the side. "I'm really glad you went with Plan B."

"Yeah." She grinned. "Me too. He totally fell for it."

Jack put his arm around her shoulders, and they walked back to the doorway. The corner desk had been knocked over and paper littered the ground. The captain had finished handcuffing Dennis, who sat on the floor.

Dennis groaned as he straightened his legs out.

"Don't move," Nelson ordered.

"Shut up, you putz," Dennis snapped. "I'm not going anywhere…" He trailed off.

Jack followed his gaze. In the middle of the scattered papers, an old red valentine stuck out.

"Patty kept the valentine," Dennis said softly. "She… she kept it." A look Jack didn't recognize crossed his face. Then he looked up. "Jack?"

"What?"

"Will you tell Patty… Tell her I love her. I always have. I just couldn't…"

Two troopers walked over to Dennis and pulled him to his feet.

Jack stared into the eyes of the man who had killed his father. Part of him wanted to draw his gun and finish his quest for vengeance then and there. He knew no one could stop him. He was too fast. Draw, safety, pull the trigger—over. Less than a fraction of a second. He could almost feel the gun kicking back in his hand. He could see Dennis crumpling to the ground as Jack unloaded the clip into him. But he could also see the look on Alice's face. The sadness. The disappointment. The pain.

What would happen to her?

Jack felt Replacement's hand slide into his.

"You're not worth killing." Jack let the words fall from his mouth.

Dennis hung his head as the troopers led him out of the room.

37

MISS ULTRA-HYPOCRITICAL

Jack tossed another bag in the Impala and headed back to the inn. The sky was a brilliant blue, and the air was crisp but not too cold. He wanted to break into a run and feel the air on his face as he walked along the gravel path. So he did. He couldn't wait to see Replacement's face.

As he pushed through the front door, three women turned. Kristine had her arm around Jack's grandmother, and Replacement held the old woman's hand.

"Jackie." Mrs. Ritter smiled and held out her arms.

Jack went over to her, and she embraced him once more.

"You promise?" She patted his cheek.

"Yes. I'll be sure to visit. Let me get things settled, and I'll be back. It's not that far."

"I'll make sure he calls," Replacement said. She had on her pink "Hope Falls" shirt with the matching baseball hat.

"You'll always have a room here," Kristine said, and gave Replacement a hug.

"Oh, nonsense," Mrs. Ritter huffed. "Next visit, they stay with me."

They all laughed and exchanged another round of hugs. Kristine kissed Jack's left cheek and Mrs. Ritter his right. Loaded down with homemade sandwiches and drinks, he and Replacement waved and walked out to the parking lot.

"I'm really going to miss it here." Replacement twirled around. "I watched the sunrise from the widow's walk this morning after you left. I don't think I've ever seen one so pretty. Where did you go?"

"I had to get a few things."

Replacement stopped short. "Oh, look!"

Jack followed her eyes to the parking lot. "What?"

"Look!" She pointed.

Jack looked again. There were only three cars in the lot: his Impala, a green sedan, and the blue Beetle. "What's wrong?"

"Someone must have rented my car!" She scooted over to the Beetle and gave it a hug.

"Wait a second, Miss Ultra-Hypocritical. You give me a hard time about the Impala, but you get to hug your car?"

"This is different. It's so cute. " She stood and sighed. "And it's not *my* car."

"Isn't it?" Jack tossed her a set of keys. "Why don't you follow me so you don't get lost."

Replacement stared down at the keys in her hand. "What is this?"

Jack just smiled.

Replacement's legs started shaking. The vibration spread up her body. "Wait. Wait just a second. Are you *serious*? You didn't. You did? *You bought me the car?*"

Jack laughed. "It's no big deal. It's pretty used, so Marty gave me a good price on it."

Replacement's mouth hung open. "Jack… How can I repay you?"

"Forget it."

"It's my car. I've never had my own car. Oh!" She raced over to Jack and threw herself into his arms, rocking back and forth. "Thank you!"

"Replacement, let me go."

She danced over to hug her new used car. She laughed and wiped her eyes as she jumped behind the wheel. "Let's go!" she shouted.

"Okay. But follow me. I need to make one stop before we head home."

38

WHAT'S MY NAME?

J ack carried the small box over and set it down on the table. Patty rocked back and forth and looked down at her hands. The doctor stood in the corner of the room, with Replacement next to him.

"Hi," Jack said as he sat down.

Patty gave him a quick wave. Her eyes darted to his face and then away.

"I wanted to stop by and see you again."

"Patty, this is Jack," the doctor said. "We talked about him this morning."

Patty looked around. Her eyes stopped on Replacement. She squinted as she stared at Replacement's pink shirt, then a little smile dawned on her face. "Hope Falls," she whispered.

Jack leaned closer. "We were just there. You grew up there."

Patty scooted forward in her chair and leaned in toward Jack. She spoke softly so the doctor couldn't hear what she said. "Steven... why did he call you Jack?"

Damn. This is going to be hard to explain.

Jack opened the box. "I picked up a couple things for you. I have some more, but they said you can only have two for right now." He pulled out a stuffed animal. It was a dog missing an ear.

"Alphie?" Patty rose partway out of her chair; her hand hovered over the toy. "It's my Alphie!"

Jack nodded. "It's yours."

She snatched it to her chest and buried her face against it. She rocked back and forth, cradling it. After a little while, the doctor stepped forward, but Jack held up a hand.

Give her some time.

Jack watched and waited. Eventually Patty looked up. Her eyes darted to the box and back down like a little kid.

Jack reached inside and took out the picture frame. Patty's mouth fell open before he'd even turned it over. Her hand flashed out and stopped as it touched his. She quickly looked away and pulled her hand back.

He set the picture frame down on the table and turned it around.

Patty inhaled and sat up straighter. "Momma."

Jack nodded.

"Momma and me."

Jack put his hands on the table and shut his eyes. After a moment, he felt her hand cover his. He opened his eyes again; something deep within him seemed to change.

Patty laid her arm flat on the table, rested her head on her arm, and stared up at him. "I'm sorry I wasn't a better mother to you."

Her words were so clear and sharp, they slammed into him.

"What?" His voice broke.

"I'm sorry I sucked at being a mother. Dragging you all over. Everything."

Jack didn't know what to say. "It—it's okay."

Tears rolled down her cheeks.

Jack swallowed. "What's my name?"

Patty wrinkled her nose. "Steven. Like your father."

Replacement softly gasped.

Jack's mother stroked the back of his hand as he sat there, stunned. "Steven?" She whispered the word.

"Yes?"

She held his hand. "Stev…" She made a face and looked away. "Sorry. It's just… hard for me."

"What's hard?" Jack asked.

"To say your name." Patty touched her heart. "It hurts. Besides Momma, Steven was the only person who was ever nice to me." She sniffled. "I guess that's why I don't say it much. I miss him."

Jack squeezed her hand. "He loved you too, Mom."

She smiled. "Thank you for bringing these." She held up Alphie.

"Sure. Next time I'll bring you some more stuff."

39

I HAD A BOOK

Jack lay in bed and stared up at the ceiling. His eyes followed the cracks, and he put his arms out to either side. Tomorrow they would move into the two-bedroom apartment downstairs.

His eyes had just closed when he heard a faint tap at the bedroom door. It opened, and Replacement's face appeared, her green eyes shining.

"You asleep?" she whispered.

"Yes."

She snorted and walked in, dragging her comforter and carrying her pillow.

Jack sat up.

"Do you want me to sleep on the couch?" he asked. "Do you want the bed?" He started to get up, but she shook her head.

"I do want the bed," she said, "but I don't want you to sleep on the couch." She looked at him nervously.

Jack raised an eyebrow.

"We can still do the pillow thing down the middle. I just don't want to sleep alone."

Jack nodded. He moved over, and she scooted up next to him.

"Thanks." She fanned the comforter out and wiggled around until she was comfortable. "You couldn't sleep?"

Jack shook his head. "I was thinking."

"About what?"

"My parents. In Florida. I haven't seen them in a while, so I'm going to go down and visit them."

"When?"

"Next month maybe. I have the time at work."

They both gazed up at the ceiling. Jack continued to follow the cracks until they faded off into the darkness.

"Would you have believed that?"

"What?" Replacement rolled onto her elbow to look at Jack.

"Patty. She said my name is Steven."

Replacement nodded, and her hand ran softly over his.

"I'm going to change my name," Jack said.

"You're not going to be Jack anymore?"

"No." He shook his head. "I'll still be Jack. That's like… who I am. It would be too weird to change that."

"Good. I like Jack."

"But I was thinking… I'm going to change it to Jack Alton Steven Stratton."

Replacement smiled at first, but then made a face.

"What?"

She fell onto her back again and pressed her lips together.

"What? You don't like the sound of that?" Jack's voice rose.

"No, I like it. I really do. I think that's very nice of you, but…" She held her hands up. "Could you go with Jack Steven Alton Stratton?"

Jack shrugged. "Why?"

"Well, if you go with it the other way… you'll be Jack A.S.S." She burst out with a laugh.

Jack's mouth fell open, then closed with a pop. He burst out laughing, too. They both lay there until their laughter faded into the occasional snicker and, finally, contented sighs.

Jack closed his eyes, and he could feel sleep clouding his thoughts.

Replacement rolled over toward him again. "How long are you going to be gone?"

"I was thinking a week with my folks. They live right outside Orlando."

Replacement was silent.

"Would you want—would you want to go with me?"

Her face scrunched up, but she still didn't answer.

"There's not much to do there; it's a retirement community. Pretty low-key, but they're not too far from Disney World. We could go to the park—"

His words were choked off, along with his air supply, as Replacement rolled on top of him. With her legs straddling his stomach, she sat up and raised her hands over her head and cheered. "Woo-hoo! I've always wanted to go. Always!" She drummed her hands on his chest.

"Well, that's sorta why I'm asking." Jack grinned.

"I know all about it. I had a book. It's not just one park. There are a bunch of different ones. It's *really cool*. Let me tell you about them…"

Jack drifted off to sleep as Replacement ran down her ever-lengthening list of the things they'd do together at Disney World.

40

IT'S ME

Jack relaxed into the front seat of the Impala and smiled. He felt great. For the past three days, all he'd done was sleep; the nightmares had stopped. And Replacement had shut off his alarm, so he'd been sleeping until almost noon.

This morning was different, though: not bad, just different. He woke up very early, and somehow he just knew what he had to do. It was as though he had made a checklist while he was sleeping, and he leapt out of bed to get started on it. He wrote a hasty note for Replacement and slipped away.

Now the Impala turned onto the road to Hope Falls. It was a long drive, but with no traffic, he made great time.

The first stop was the library. One lone interior light was on inside, but he could tell it was closed. He sighed as he walked up to the entrance and looked in. He could almost feel the calmness and smell the wood.

Maybe I'll stop back after I see my grandmother.

Jack grinned. He was looking forward to his surprise visit. He'd decided to come only this morning, so he hadn't called, but he was sure she wouldn't mind.

Jack opened the book return chute. He looked down at the wrapped package in his hands and smiled. Inside were the two yearbooks, and an apology card from Replacement for "accidentally" borrowing them. She'd found them when they were unpacking and had wanted to drive back right then. He'd told her he'd take care of it.

As he slid the package inside and closed the door, he suppressed the urge to pick up the phone and thank her. Before she'd wrapped up the yearbooks, he'd taken another look at his parents' photos—and when he opened the book to Patty's photo, he saw that the graffiti someone had written about her was gone. The paper was a little worn there now, but otherwise you wouldn't know anyone had ever defaced it.

Replacement never said a word.

She's good like that.

Jack ran his hand through his hair and headed back to the car. The Impala restarted with a deep roar, and Jack smiled and patted the dashboard. She'd been running even better since Marty had flushed her out. He slipped her into drive and headed back down the road.

When he hit the gas, the Impala purred, and he settled back into the seat to enjoy the feeling as the car softly rose and fell and the speed increased. His fingers gripped the wheel lightly, and he listened to the engine hum.

Is this content or happy? Maybe it's both?

He pulled the rearview mirror down. A man who needed a shave stared back. Jack smiled and flipped the mirror back up.

He was about to push the pedal to the floor when he saw the sign up ahead. He let the car slow way down before he pulled in. His head swiveled around in a full scan, but he knew he was alone.

The Hope Falls Cemetery was set on a few acres of carefully maintained ground. Large trees ringed the edges, and in the middle, a huge oak rose up, its thick branches spread out.

Jack could feel his muscles tighten as a somberness seeped in. He looked from the small headstones to a statue of a weeping angel draped over a tomb, its wings hanging in perpetual sorrow. He turned his head away at the sight of a lone teddy bear against a grave.

Jack tried to look straight ahead as he drove the narrow road to the back left corner. He never did well with death, and in his twenty-six years he'd seen more than most. A gallery of faces flashed at the edges of his thoughts.

None of us make it out of here alive.

When he reached the back, he stopped and shut the car off. He was grateful that Kristine had told him right where it was, so he didn't have to search. He made his way down a slightly worn path; he was certain it had been made by Kristine and his grandmother, on their trips to the little headstone.

His father was buried beside his grandfather. On the granite marker were the words: BELOVED SON. STEVEN RITTER.

Two weeks ago, I didn't even know him. Now...

Jack hung his head and stood silently. The first breeze of the morning stirred the grass.

"Hi, Dad. It's me, Steven..."

EPILOGUE – GATHERING DARKNESS

As still as the mannequin beside her, Marisa peered out of the window of her tattoo parlor at the silver sedan parked across the street. Its dark-tinted windows hid its occupants. Like a little girl at the edge of the cellar stairs, looking into the dark, she felt the urge to turn and run wash over her. She didn't know why, but she had the feeling someone was watching her.

What if they find me…? I can't go back to that living hell again.

She tried to shake all the old, terrifying, paranoid thoughts from her head. She reached up and turned off the neon OPEN sign. As if connected to the same switch, the sedan's headlights snapped on at the same moment, and then it pulled away from the curb. She watched intently as the taillights disappeared down the road.

"Marisa?" Joey called to her from behind the counter, breaking her from her trance.

Marisa didn't turn around as she locked the front door. She tried to drive the old fears away. *No one knows who I really am,* she reminded herself. Still, even after all these years, she couldn't stop looking over her shoulder.

Joey thrust his large tattooed arms deep into his pockets. "Ah… Marisa?" He looked more like an awkward teen than the tough guy he usually pretended to be. "Is there any chance I could have tomorrow night off?"

Marisa raised an eyebrow as she walked over to the register. "That's three days this week."

"I know. But I need it, and Shawn can't cover. It's kinda important."

"Just kinda?" Hiding a smile, Marisa cashed out the register. She knew she'd cover for him, but she wasn't going to say yes right away. She had to perpetuate her reputation as a hard-nosed businesswoman.

"No, it's big." Joey leaned against the counter, and that goofy I'm-in-love smile that had been appearing regularly on his face showed up again. "I'm having dinner at Rosalie's. With her parents. First time," he added.

Marisa's face remained neutral as she continued to cash out. She was happy for him. Those little rituals make up a normal life. Somewhere deep inside her chest, the empty ache hurt a little more. How she would have liked a little normal. To bring someone home to meet her parents…

"Marisa?"

"Sure. I've got you covered."

"Yes!" Joey pumped his fist as if he had just made a game-winning shot.

"I take it that things are going well with Rosalie?"

"Un-flippin'-believably good. She's… We talk about everything." Joey's head tipped to the side. "What about you?"

"Me?" Marisa walked over to the coffee machine and filled a thermos with some hot cocoa.

"Yeah. It's like a parade of guys keep coming in, tripping over their tongues to ask you out, but you shoot them down right from the word 'go.'"

Marisa huffed and put a hand on her hip.

"You do!" Joey pressed. "It's like a running joke. A guy comes in and asks you out, and you're like, 'NO!' Cutting him off like a guillotine."

"I do not."

"You do. Julie and I were cracking up guessing where the guy today would have taken you. I picked the symphony, and she thought some wine tasting thing."

"The guy in the Audi?" Marisa laughed. "Since he couldn't take his eyes off my chest, I'd have a different guess about where he wanted to go."

"Not every guy is a creep…" Joey traced an invisible outline on the counter. "What about the cop?" He floated out the question without looking up. "That Jack guy."

When Marisa didn't answer, Joey peeked up at her. Her lips were pressed in a firm line. Her brown eyes were as dark and cold as the night outside.

Joey stepped back from the counter and swallowed. "I, ah… I just… He seems like—"

She cut him off. "Let me know how your dinner goes." She opened the small refrigerator and took out a wrapped ham and cheese sandwich.

Joey sighed. "Sorry if I overstepped," he mumbled as he slipped out the back door.

As Marisa stood alone in the tattoo parlor, that ache in her chest grew a little bigger again. *Jack.* The name hurt. It hurt to hear it. Thinking about him hurt even more.

Like a child, she hurried over to the closed door and stared hopefully out into the darkness, expecting him to walk around the corner at that instant. Jack had been assigned foot patrol downtown. She stood there looking out as a few snowflakes fell past the street light.

"Tu sei il bello mio," she whispered to the night. "You're my beautiful one."

She grabbed the thermos and sandwich, turned off the light, and headed out the back. The heavy metal exit door closed behind her with a loud bang.

The back alley was well lit, and Marisa always made sure it stayed clean. Even the garbage bin and recycling container were neatly arranged. The space between the buildings was just wide enough to back a truck down, but tonight it was empty.

Marisa started down the alley. Darkened rear doorways and alcoves dotted the wall to the right, and she peered into each recess. She gingerly switched the sandwich to her right hand, careful not to squish it with the thermos.

The next alcove was covered in shadows. Only one of the three lights above the little loading area was still on. She hesitated. An errant snowflake landed on the back of her neck, and she shivered.

Footsteps behind her made her jump. She turned.

A thin homeless man shuffled down the alley straight toward her. A thick, worn jacket flared out around him. Beneath the coat was a rainbow of different cloths and materials.

He slowed to a stop in front of her. His fingers twitched at his sides, and his upper body rocked slightly back and forth.

"Who's there?" The man ran his hand down his unkempt beard. Wild brown and gray hair poked out from underneath a brown knit cap pulled low. From behind round glasses, he gazed at Marisa with hungry eyes, but his eyebrows pulled together warily.

"Hi, Thaddeus. It's me, Marisa." She held out the sandwich and thermos.

"Oh." A broad smile crossed his face, and his cheeks flushed r
Vitagliano." He reached out eagerly and took the gifts. "I really
enough."

"It's nothing."

"It is to me." Thaddeus looked at the ground.

"Are you sure you don't want to go to the shelter tonight? It's going to be cold."

Thaddeus shook his head and moved closer. Marisa tried not to wrinkle her nose at the smell. "I got layers." He pulled at his thick, worn jacket.

"Well, if you get too cold, be sure to head over." Marisa smiled, turned, and walked on.

"Will do, Ms. Vitagliano." He waved, then darted into a darkened doorway with his meal. "Thanks again," he called out.

Marisa wrapped her arms around her waist as she made her way down the alley. The whole stretch ahead was pitch black. She frowned. She had just had the landlord fix that light. She made a mental note to take care of it tomorrow.

As she neared the darkness, she stopped. Snowflakes floated down around her face, but something else drifted on the cold wind, too. The faintest whiff of cologne reached her nose. Bile rose up in her throat.

They say the strongest memories are not visual, but scent. And that smell resurrected a life that she thought she had left buried in the past. Images slammed into her mind as she thought about that day she couldn't forget. The day when everything good she knew died. She shook. In her mind's eye, she could see his face once more.

"Hello, Angelica."

A man in an H. Huntsman suit walked out of the shadows.

"It's been a long time."

Marisa trembled. She'd seen this killer's face in her dreams a thousand times, but it had been years since she'd heard his voice. It cut deep. Old wounds ripped open, and terror held her fast.

A malevolent grin spread across the man's face as he strode toward her. The heels of his expensive shoes on the tar sounded like gunshots to her ears. With each step, she flinched.

From some memory long since buried, she heard another voice, screaming to her from the past: "Run, Angelica! Run!"

She turned to flee—but another man rushed out from the darkness and grabbed her. Her scream was cut off as a rag was clamped over her mouth. As she inhaled the fumes, the last thing she remembered was him…

JACKS ARE WILD

Find out what happens next in the next thrilling installment: *Jacks Are Wild*

Handsome white knight Jack Stratton is back in this action-packed, thrilling adventure. When his sexy old flame disappears, no one thinks it's suspicious, except Jack and one unbalanced witness. Jack feels in his gut that something is wrong. He knows Marisa has a past, and if it ever caught up with her… it would be deadly.

Determined to buck the critics and listen to his instincts, he and his feisty young sidekick plunge ahead and start tracking down leads, hoping to find Marisa in time. The trail leads them into all sorts of trouble, and lands them smack in the middle of an all-out mob war between the Italian Mafia and the Japanese Yakuza. When evidence surfaces that Marisa was kidnapped, Jack must navigate through the warring parties, assassins, and cold-blooded hit men to outwit the cunning kidnappers before it's too late. As the body count rises, the stakes in this game are life and death—with no rules except one—Jacks are Wild.

THE DETECTIVE JACK STRATTON MYSTERY-THRILLER SERIES

The Detective Jack Stratton Mystery-Thriller Series, authored by *Wall Street Journal* bestselling writer Christopher Greyson, has over 5,000 five-star reviews and over one million readers and counting. If you'd love to read another page-turning thriller with mystery, humor, and a dash of romance, pick up the next book in the highly acclaimed series today.

AND THEN SHE WAS GONE

A hometown hero with a heart of gold, Jack Stratton was raised in a whorehouse by his prostitute mother. Jack seemed destined to become another statistic, but now his life has taken a turn for the better. Determined to escape his past, he's headed for a career in law enforcement. When his foster mother asks him to look into a girl's disappearance, Jack quickly gets drawn into a baffling mystery. As Jack digs deeper, everyone becomes a suspect—including himself. Caught between the criminals and the cops, can Jack discover the truth in time to save the girl? Or will he become the next victim?

GIRL JACKED

Guilt has driven a wedge between Jack and the family he loves. When Jack, now a police officer, hears the news that his foster sister Michelle is missing, it cuts straight to his core. The police think she just took off, but Jack knows Michelle would never leave her loved ones behind—like he did. Forced to confront the demons from his past, Jack must take action, find Michelle, and bring her home... or die trying.

JACK KNIFED

Constant nightmares have forced Jack to seek answers about his rough childhood and the dark secrets hidden there. The mystery surrounding Jack's birth father leads Jack to investigate the twenty-seven-year-old murder case in Hope Falls.

JACKS ARE WILD

When Jack's sexy old flame disappears, no one thinks it's suspicious except Jack and one unbalanced witness. Jack feels in his gut that something is wrong. He knows that Marisa has a past, and if it ever caught up with her—it would be deadly. The trail leads him into all sorts of trouble—landing him smack in the middle of an all-out mob war between the Italian Mafia and the Japanese Yakuza.

JACK AND THE GIANT KILLER

Rogue hero Jack Stratton is back in another action-packed, thrilling adventure. While recovering from a gunshot wound, Jack gets a seemingly harmless private investigation job—locate the owner of a lost dog—Jack begrudgingly assists. Little does he know it will place him directly in the crosshairs of a merciless serial killer.

DATA JACK

In this digital age of hackers, spyware, and cyber terrorism—data is more valuable than gold. Thieves plan to steal the keys to the digital kingdom and with this much money at stake, they'll kill for it. Can Jack and Alice (aka Replacement) stop the pack of ruthless criminals before they can *Data Jack?*

JACK OF HEARTS

When his mother and the members of her neighborhood book club ask him to catch the "Orange Blossom Cove Bandit," a small-time thief who's stealing garden gnomes and peace of mind from their quiet retirement community, how can Jack refuse? The peculiar mystery proves to be more than it appears, and things take a deadly turn. Now, Jack finds it's up to him to stop a crazed killer, save his parents, and win the hand of the girl he loves—but if he survives, will it be Jack who ends up with a broken heart?

JACK FROST

Jack has a new assignment: to investigate the suspicious death of a soundman on the hit TV show *Planet Survival.* Jack goes undercover as a security agent where the show is filming on nearby Mount Minuit. Soon trapped on the treacherous peak by a blizzard, a mysterious killer continues to stalk the cast and crew of *Planet Survival.* What started out as a game is now a deadly competition for survival. As the temperature drops and the body count rises, what will get them first? The mountain or the killer?

Hear your favorite characters come to life
in audio versions of the
Detective Jack Stratton Mystery-Thriller Series!
Audio Books now available on Audible!

Novels featuring Jack Stratton in order:
AND THEN SHE WAS GONE
GIRL JACKED
JACK KNIFED
JACKS ARE WILD
JACK AND THE GIANT KILLER
DATA JACK
JACK OF HEARTS
JACK FROST

Psychological Thriller
THE GIRL WHO LIVED
Ten years ago, four people were brutally murdered. One girl lived. As the anniversary of the murders approaches, Faith Winters is released from the psychiatric hospital and yanked back to the last spot on earth she wants to be—her hometown where the slayings took place. Wracked by the lingering echoes of survivor's guilt, Faith spirals into a black hole of alcoholism and wanton self-destruction. Finding no solace at the bottom of a bottle, Faith decides to track down her sister's killer—and then discovers that she's the one being hunted.

Epic Fantasy
PURE OF HEART
Orphaned and alone, rogue-teen Dean Walker has learned how to take care of himself on the rough city streets. Unjustly wanted by the police, he takes refuge within the shadows of the city. When Dean stumbles upon an old man being mugged, he tries to help—only to discover that the victim is anything but helpless and far more than he appears. Together with three friends, he sets out on an epic quest where only the pure of heart will prevail.

ACKNOWLEDGMENTS

I would like to thank all the wonderful readers out there. It's you who make the literary world what it is today—a place of dreams filled with tales of adventure. To all of you who have taken Jack and Replacement under your wings and spread the word via social media and who have spent the time to go back and write a great review, I say THANK YOU! Your efforts keep the characters alive and give me the encouragement and time to keep writing. I can't thank YOU enough.

Word of mouth is crucial for any author to succeed. If you enjoy the series, please consider letting others know or leaving a review at Amazon, even if it is only a line or two; it would make all the difference and I would appreciate it very much.

I would also like to thank my wife. She's the best wife, mother, and my partner in crime. She is an invaluable content editor and I could not do this without her!

My thanks also go out to: my two awesome kids, my dear mother, my family, my fantastic editors—David Gatewood of Lone Trout Editing, Faith Williams of The Atwater Group, and Karen Lawson and Janet Hitchcock of The Proof is in the Reading. My fabulous proofreader—Charlie Wilson of Landmark Editorial. My unbelievably helpful beta readers, Kay Bloomberg, and my two awesome kids.

ABOUT THE AUTHOR

My name is Christopher Greyson, and I am a storyteller.

Since I was a little boy, I have dreamt of what mystery was around the next corner, or what quest lay over the hill. If I couldn't find an adventure, one usually found me, and now I weave those tales into my stories. I am blessed to have written the bestselling Detective Jack Stratton Mystery-Thriller Series. The collection includes *And Then She Was GONE, Girl Jacked, Jack Knifed, Jacks Are Wild, Jack and the Giant Killer, Data Jack, Jack of Hearts, Jack Frost,* with *Jack of Diamonds* due later this year. I have also penned the bestselling psychological thriller, *The Girl Who Lived* and a special collection of mysteries, *The Adventures of Finn and Annie.*

My background is an eclectic mix of degrees in theatre, communications, and computer science. Currently I reside in Massachusetts with my lovely wife and two fantastic children. My wife, Katherine Greyson, who is my chief content editor, is an author of her own romance series, *Everyone Keeps Secrets.*

My love for tales of mystery and adventure began with my grandfather, a decorated World War I hero. I will never forget being introduced to his friend, a WWI pilot who flew across the skies at the same time as the feared, legendary Red Baron. My love of reading and storytelling eventually led me to write *Pure of Heart*, a young adult fantasy that I released in 2014.

I love to hear from my readers. Please visit ChristopherGreyson.com, where you can become a preferred reader and enjoy additional FREE *Adventures of Finn and Annie*, advanced notifications of book releases and more! Thank you for reading my novels. I hope my stories have brightened your day.

Sincerely,

CPSIA information can be obtained
at www.ICGtesting.com
Printed in the USA
LVHW090427280720
661633LV00007B/617

9 781683 990307